THE
Summersby Island
HOUSE

WENDY DEWAR HUGHES
SUZANNE LIEURANCE

CREATIVE CARAVAN PRESS

THE
Summersby Island
HOUSE

WENDY DEWAR HUGHES
SUZANNE LIEURANCE

Chapter One

The letter lay on the table where it had been flung the evening before—face up, with the usual twin folds. This was the third such letter in the past two years. Worded in bland business-speak, it gave almost no indication of the upheaval that would follow, the same kind that had resulted from the previous two.

Lana Stewart barely gave it a glance as she dashed to the kitchen to pour coffee into her insulated travel mug. Thinking about what it said would have to wait until after work. She grabbed the strap of her oversized purse, flung it over her shoulder as she wrapped a scarf around her neck, and locked the front door of her apartment on her way out.

The rest of the bank staff had wandered into the boardroom and were just taking their seats when Lana slipped in. She flipped her scarf onto the back of a chair, sat down next to Owen Sheffield and took the last sip of her coffee.

"Just in time," Owen said dryly. He pushed his wire-framed glasses up the bridge of his nose with his middle finger. Lana gave him a tight smile. She had tried hard to like him but, as the branch know-it-all, Owen had the uncanny ability to irritate by his mere presence.

Branch manager, Sally McCardle, stood up and called the regular Monday morning meeting to order. Her shock-platinum hair crowned her head in a messy bun, drawing attention by contrast to the cherry-red lipstick she wore every day. With twelve other staff slouched in chairs around the table, it was easy to see that no one was thrilled to be there at 8:00 a.m. to listen to the latest news on interest rates and retirement savings plans. Lana stifled a yawn and rested her forehead on the back of her hand, pretending to be taking notes.

A sharp heel connected with her shin and Lana let out a muffled squeak. Across the table, her friend, Sherry Michaels, lifted an eyebrow and smirked. Lana glared back. *Okay*, she thought with a sigh, *I'll try to look enthusiastic.*

Fifteen minutes later, the meeting wrapped up. The staff pushed back chairs and drifted off to their respective stations. Lana grabbed her scarf and purse and headed for her office, catching up with Sherry in the hallway.

"What was the kick for?" she asked. "I think you took a gouge out of my shin."

"You'll survive that more easily than you would have a warning from Sally," Sherry said. "You know she's been on the war path lately about numbers and I think she may have you in her sights."

"Why? I can't help it if no one wants to borrow money. What am I supposed to do—stand on the street corner and lift the hem of my skirt?"

Sherry snorted. "With legs like yours it probably wouldn't hurt, but I don't think that is the desired effect," she drawled. "The main idea is that we both have to do everything we can to get money into the hands of local businesses while at the same time making sure every deal is ironclad. I know. Impossible."

Sherry tucked a bouncy brown curl behind her left ear and turned into her own office across a gray hallway from Lana's. "Don't forget you're still on probation for another month," she added before closing her office door.

Lana hadn't forgotten. When the large investment firm she had worked for in Chicago had been taken over by another gigantic firm, she and a hundred or so others had found themselves looking at pink slips and emptying their desks within minutes of hearing the news. It had happened that fast. She had even started showing up for work early so the powers that be would know she had serious designs on a promotion. Instead, she'd been ushered into the conference room with everyone else, informed that her position had been terminated as of immediately, and instructed to go clean out her desk and hand in her badge. *So much for climbing the ladder of success,* she had thought as she tossed the meager contents of her desk into a plastic bag.

That had been three months ago and happened to coincide with the day Carl Jenkins—the third, no less—her almost-fiancé, had informed her that he didn't think it was working out between them and he needed a little breathing space. Breathing space also included his new assistant, a leggy blonde named Sonya. Lana had anticipated receiving a diamond ring any day. Instead he had marched into her office as she gathered up her coat and purse and had broken up with her before she could get out the door.

By the time Lana got back to her apartment, the mail had arrived. Once she'd managed to dig her mailbox keys from the bottom of her purse, collect the letters, and unlock the front door, she dropped the bag of office gleanings on her tiny kitchen table and sifted through the mail.

Then she froze. She recognized the return address on one of the letters. It was from the management company that looked after her building. "Looked after" was putting it kindly. Lana slit the envelope open with a kitchen knife, expecting to find a rent increase. Her eyes traveled down the body of the letter and she realized she was looking at an eviction notice instead. According to the letter, the building owners had decided to make major renovations and sell the apartments as condos. They included a shiny brochure offering her the opportunity to purchase one of the resulting condos but first she had to move out. Lana tossed the brochure in the trash. She wouldn't miss this dump, any more than she had missed the last one that had evicted her for similar purposes.

When her job had still showed potential, she might have considered buying one of those newly renovated condos after the second eviction. But since that had fallen through with one handshake in a boardroom, her dream of home ownership had turned to dust.

When the initial shock of her horrible day subsided, Lana sat down on the edge of her second-hand sofa and sobbed. Talk about a triple whammy! She had lost her job, her boyfriend and her apartment all on the same day. Between sniffles, she picked up the phone and called her old friend, Sherry, in Florida.

"Listen," Sherry said after Lana stopped blubbering into the telephone. "Why don't you come home to Summersby Island? My branch manager told me this morning they're thinking of adding another loans officer to the staff. I'll put in a good word for you if you like."

Six days later, after giving away most of her household belongings and packing her suitcases, Lana boarded a flight for Florida. As she gazed out the plane window over snow-covered Chicago, she blew a good-bye kiss to the city below and settled into her seat. She closed her eyes and allowed her thoughts to roam the place of her childhood, the island to which she thought she would never return. In her mind's eye she could see the palm trees swaying in the offshore breezes and could almost feel the warm sand between her toes as she wandered the shoreline searching for shells.

Before leaving Chicago, Lana had called ahead to the island and made a reservation at The Summersby Motel, a bright little motel that had been there as long as she could remember. Her flight landed in Orlando and she picked up the rental car at the airport. She popped the trunk open and tossed in two suitcases containing everything she owned in the world. If she hurried, she could make the five o'clock ferry. *All bridges already burned*, she thought as she headed west toward the coast.

The next morning after a long, deep sleep, Lana threw open the door of her quaint and cozy motel room and drew in a magnificent breath of fresh sea air. Sunlight glinted off rippling waves, setting the turquoise waters aglow with millions of sparkling crystals. Overhead a gull squawked a pointless complaint, scanning for easy spoils. Before her, a path to the beach beckoned. Lana threw on a t-shirt and a pair of capris, then thrust her feet into the orange flip-flops she bought at a shop in the airport the day before. As she stepped out into the dazzling light, she flung her arms open to the rising sun and cried, "And this is February! Why did I ever leave?"

True to her word, Sherry had recommended Lana for the new position at the local bank, Summersby Savings. It wasn't going to make her rich or famous and there was no ladder to climb, but Lana couldn't remember when she had been more thankful to be hired. That had been two months before.

Now, in her shoebox of an office, Lana stuffed her purse into a cupboard next to her desk and wiggled her computer mouse. She checked her appointment calendar on the bank's network and frowned at the screen. Only one potential customer was scheduled to see her. If she didn't get her numbers up soon, her position might be in jeopardy. She couldn't bear the thought of one more thing not panning out.

She thought of the letter lying on her table in the rental she had taken when she first arrived on Summersby Island. Three days in the local motel, charming as it was, convinced her that eating out every night would excavate serious holes in her financial reserves. She answered an ad in the local paper and took an upstairs apartment in a house on the edge of town, but as the eviction letter pointed out, the owners now wanted the apartment for their daughter so Lana would have to find alternative accommodations.

Lana had another fleeting thought about standing on street corners showing her calves. Then with a shake of her head that sent a long, auburn curl tumbling over her forehead, she tossed that thought from her mind.

Lana heard a tap on her office door and looked up to see Sherry standing there. "I know you have an appointment soon but I have to show you this." Sherry stepped into Lana's office and tossed a sheet of paper on Lana's desk.

Lana turned it around to read. "What is it?"

"A foreclosure. I know you found a place to rent but this is a steal. Are you interested?"

"In buying a house?" Lana examined the details on the paper. "This is amazing."

"I know," Sherry agreed. "Beach houses almost never come on the market here."

"No. I mean the timing. I got an eviction notice yesterday. The landlord wants my apartment for his daughter." Lana's eyes slid down to the bottom of the sheet. "And the price is…" She gasped.

"You can do it. Tell Sally you want it before they do anything else. You can decide after you've seen it if you want to let it go."

Lana looked up. "Will the bank give me a mortgage though? The down payment would take all my savings."

"I know the house," Sherry said. "It's out on Sandpiper Road. It needs work but you can probably add in what you'll need when you apply for the financing." She turned to go. "I'm serious—don't wait. This one will get snapped up."

Lana checked the time. She had ten minutes until her appointment.

Chapter Two

Lana was studying the details of the house when she was startled from her calculations by a man who strode into her office without knocking. He was tall, with sawdust-covered dark curls escaping from under a ball cap with *DiMarco's Marina* embroidered on the front. His muscled arms strained against the rolled-up sleeves of a blue plaid shirt. The man wore jeans and work boots and a knife sheath hung from his belt. Lana noticed the receptionist, Jessica, behind him. Jessica shrugged, spread her hands and walked away shaking her head.

Lana jumped to her feet and rounded her desk, her hand extended. The man gave it a perfunctory shake.

"McClaren, Jason," he said. "Everyone calls me Mack."

"Hello, Mr. McClaren," Lana answered.

"Mack."

"I'm Lana Stewart. Please have a seat, Mack." She said his name deliberately. It paid to get things off on the right foot, especially when signing this client might mean keeping her job. "How may I help you today?"

Mack eyed her levelly for a moment as though sizing her up. His hazel eyes, more brown than green, sparkled and were rimmed by long, dark lashes. Lana sat up straighter. Mack pulled the cap from his head, releasing a shower of sawdust, and sat back. "I've got a big job I'm bidding on and I need some interim financing. What I've got in place here isn't enough to cover materials and extra labor for the duration."

"All right," Lana said evenly. "What kind of work do you do, Mr. McClaren?" She saw his eyes narrow. "I mean Mack. Tell me about your business."

"Construction, building, renovations," he replied. "There's supposed to be a new hotel project going in along the beach and I plan to bid on it. But first I need to know I can get the cash I need, when I need it. Have you heard about the hotel?"

Lana shook her head. "I'm sorry, no. But I haven't been living on Summersby Island for long. This time, anyway."

"Meaning?"

"I lived here as a child." She tucked a strand of hair behind one ear. "I've been living in Chicago for the past few years." She didn't want him to know how many years, since that would give away her age, and at thirty-two and still single, she thought she needed every advantage she could hang onto. She already knew from the data on Mack's account that he was thirty-four.

For the next forty-five minutes, Lana discussed possible options for financing Mack's new project.

"It's not a done deal," he said as he leaned his forearms on the front of her desk and stared at the computer monitor. "So tell me the most you can give me, provided everything goes through."

The sun-bleached hair on his powerful arms sparkled and Lana wanted to reach out and touch it. With effort, she dragged her attention back to the figures swimming before her eyes.

She shook her head. "I really want to help you, Mack, but I'm going to have to speak to the Branch Manager before I can give you an answer."

He stood and clapped the ball cap on his head. "Well then, let me know what you figure out. But make it quick, will you? I've got employees waiting to see if they're going to have work next week." Before she could reply, he marched out, leaving her watching his back side as he left.

Sherry tapped a knuckle on the door. "You can shut your mouth now." She grinned. "I think you're starting to drool."

Lana closed her mouth and smoothed her hair. "No, I'm not!"

"He's something, isn't he?" said Sherry. "The back view is as good as the front. If I weren't married to Tim, I'd fish him out of the pond in a Florida minute."

Lana blinked.

"Earth calling Lana," Sherry said, waving her hand in front of Lana's eyes.

"I have got to get him this loan," Lana declared, moving papers around on her desk.

"Mmm, yeah, but I think I should warn you. If you're setting your sights on him, Mack McClaren is what you might call gun-shy—as in, allergic to women. He got dumped at the altar a couple of years ago when his bride-to-be ran off with someone else."

"That seems to be going around," Lana said. She dropped into her chair. "After the unfortunate demise of my romance with Carl Jenkins III, I'm a little gun-shy myself. By the way, what did you come in here for?"

Sherry pulled a chair up close to the other side of the desk and slid into it. "I want to know what happened with the house. Did you talk to Sally?"

Lana's eyes lit up. "I can go look at it after work today," she said. "Come with me."

The house stood at the west side of the island, facing the sunset on Abigail Beach. Lana drove slowly along West Beach Loop checking out the neighborhood. A lot had changed since she left the island partway through junior high school. Like most of her fellow students, she couldn't wait to leave behind the rinky-dink town where everyone's mother knew what you were up to at any time of the day or night. Now, coming back after all these years, it felt like slipping into an old sweater—comfortable, welcoming, and well-worn.

"Does Emily Shipner still live there?" Lana asked Sherry as they crept past a lime green clapboard house edging the beach.

"She died a couple years ago," Sherry replied. "I think she had a stroke."

"Oh," Lana said. She suddenly felt like the loss was hers, too.

Sherry pointed. "The house is just up ahead. It's the one with the palm tree by the drive."

Lana pulled her car into the sandy track that barely resembled a driveway. Weeds and patches of scrubby grass grew up between the twin tracks. She turned off the engine and got out of the car. Sherry got out too and stood on her side of the vehicle.

"I don't think it's been lived in for quite a while," Sherry said. She picked her way in high heels through the tangle matting the small yard. "This house is real old Florida style."

Lana tilted her head to the side. "Is that roof crooked or is it me?"

Sherry stopped tiptoeing and balanced on one foot. "It's crooked."

On one side of the house, a pile of old tires lay draped in dead foliage dropped from a bedraggled overhead palm. The middle tread of the wood slat steps leading up to a veranda that spanned the house's width had split in three. Paint peeled, veranda railings sagged, and the metal roof had not seen good days in a long while.

Lana glanced at Sherry who promptly pasted on a cheery grin and suggested, "We might as well look inside, seeing as we're already here."

Lana took a deep breath, exhaled slowly and strode toward the house. She jumped over the broken steps and reached back to give Sherry a hand up. "If the key works, that is," said Lana. The screen door, minus screens, creaked eerily as Lana pulled it open. Sliding the key into the lock was easy but required a fair amount of jiggling and lip biting to make it turn. She pushed the door open slowly, in case a flock of bats might come screaming out. That didn't happen so she tiptoed inside, clutching Sherry's wrist.

"It's not as bad as I expected," Sherry said. She peered around a corner into a tiny living room. Scraps of stained and faded wallpaper hung from the walls and a truly horrible green shag carpet, worn down to the webbing, covered the floor. "The walls don't even slump," Sherry added.

Lana looked at her. "I guess that's one plus. I don't care what anyone says though, this carpet has to go." The two women laughed and turned down the hallway. "Let's see what the kitchen has to offer."

That room had evidently received visitors of the fur and feather variety as droppings and other debris littered the curling linoleum floor. An avocado green fridge stood against one wall, its door open. "I don't even want to imagine what was in this," Lana said, using two fingertips to pick up a cardboard carton from the refrigerator shelf then gingerly returning it. The harvest gold stove sported a coating of black spills and the oven door sagged open like an old man's mouth.

"Gosh," Sherry said, "these colors are from my childhood. I wonder how long these appliances have been here."

"Since before you were born, no doubt," Lana answered. "Who lived in this place anyway and how come it has been so badly let go?"

"From what I heard, an old man owned it. He lived alone and had a couple of adult kids who lived somewhere else in the country. When he died they fought over it for a few years until either they got tired of the whole thing or the lawyers ending up with all the money. There was a lien on the property, and when nobody made payments, the ownership reverted to the bank. They don't want it, which is why the selling price is so low. It's pretty unusual to find beachfront property here without having relatives all the way back to Captain Summersby." She thumped on a wall with her knuckles in a few places. "You'll want to have an inspector take a look at it and see if it's salvageable. It looks pretty sturdy, even if it is filthy."

They toured the two small bedrooms with miniscule closets and a bathroom with a claw-foot tub and plumbed-in shower. A tiny hexagonal window looked out on the side of the house.

"Since we've saved the best for last," Lana said, "we'd better check out the back yard." A sliding glass door with tracks so gritty she could barely open it led out onto a large patio made of poured concrete. Unlike most other areas of the house, this part looked fairly new. Beyond the patio stretched a scrubby tract of sand and grass and beyond it, the beach. The sugary sand glowed pale gold in the lowering sun and Lana and Sherry both stopped and stared. Turquoise water, now toned teal in the slanting light, rolled in ruffled waves onto the tranquil shore.

"It's like heaven here," Lana said. "Why is no one on the beach?"

"Have you forgotten? It's winter. Only northerners go to the beach in the winter."

"I'm a transplanted northerner. Come on. Take your heels off and let's go get our feet wet.

The Summersby Island House

Chapter Three

"Tell me about him," Sherry prodded. The two of them strolled along the water's edge, carrying their shoes and checking out the neighborhood lining the beach next to what Lana had already begun to consider her house. A few lights had come on down the beach but otherwise all was quiet. A curious gull flew overhead, scouting for food but didn't stick around. Now, as the sun sank into the sea, the two women went back and sat on the edge of the patio, watching the sky turn scarlet and mauve. Lana pushed her hands through her long, loopy curls and twisted them together at the nape of her neck. With a sigh, she dropped her head onto her arms, which rested across her knees.

"Carl Jenkins? I thought he was going to propose," Lana said. She looked up and plucked at the hem of her skirt. "I thought he was wonderful—'the one' you know. Everything had been going so well. He treated me like a queen and he even took me home to meet his parents. They're such nice people and they live in big house in an upscale area of the city. I had started looking at wedding gowns, stopping in front of the store windows. One Saturday morning I went out shopping with a girlfriend from work. At first we just window-shopped; then I got up the nerve to try a few dresses on. That's how sure I was."

"He really hurt you, didn't he?" Sherry said softly. She laid a gentle hand on Lana's shoulder.

Lana blinked back the tears she didn't want to cry and nodded. "Yeah, he did." She drew a tissue from her purse and blew her nose. "I thought I would finally have a home again, and a real family. Relatives, kids, Christmas dinners."

"Listen, I know it feels bad now but you'll have better days, I promise." She gave Lana a sympathetic smile and pulled her into a hug. "Enough about him now, okay? What about the house? Here's your chance to have a home that's really your own. Are you going to take it? It has potential, don't you think?"

Lana sat up straighter and looked up at the overhang that would shade the patio on hot summer days. The house would need a lot of work but if she planned to stay on Summersby Island, she didn't have a lot of choices. Rentals on Summersby Island were few and far between and to buy anything else was out of the question. The prices on most homes were beyond her reach. The thought of actually owning her own place had never really occurred to her before, but now that it was a possibility she felt a little bubble of excitement start from somewhere deep inside.

"It could be really cute, couldn't it?" Lana stood and surveyed the beach side of the house. "It needs a bit of propping up and definitely some decorating TLC but if I can swing the financials and find a contractor, yes, I think I'll get it. It will probably take all my savings for the down payment."

"You might not have to use all your savings. The bank wants it off their hands so they'll probably negotiate. They're not in the housing business; they're in the money lending business. And as a bank employee, I'm sure you can swing a sweetheart of a deal."

Lana linked an arm through her friend's. "Let's go home. I've got a big day tomorrow. I have to start packing."

The management at the bank were so anxious to unload what they considered a derelict old building they jumped at the chance to get it easily off their books. Lana knew the property had value because lots on Summersby Island didn't go cheaply, so when a bit of haggling on the price produced a number she could live with, she signed the papers.

Lana almost skipped back to her office. She tapped on Sherry's door and waved the handful of paperwork. "Guess who you're looking at?" She didn't wait for an answer. "The proud owner of one dilapidated beach house. Can you believe it?"

Sherry jumped from her chair and threw her arms around Lana. "What did I tell you? Did you get a good deal?"

"Incredibly good. And possession is right away. I can't move in yet, of course, until I convince the birds and mice to find other lodgings, but I can start working on it right away. I don't have to be out of the apartment I'm renting until the end of the month, so that gives me two whole weeks." She drew in a deep breath. "Oh, my goodness! What can I do in only two weeks? I don't even know a carpenter here anymore."

"Didn't you just have a loan interview with a contractor? Maybe he could help you. What was his name?" Sherry hid a grin behind her hand.

"Jack...no, Jason." Lana frowned. "I remember now. He introduced himself as Mack. But he wanted the money to build a hotel. I doubt he'd have time to fix my deck rails."

Sherry shrugged and settled back into her office chair. "You could always ask. Tim's got a pal on town council and scuttlebutt says they probably won't allow any big chain hotels on the island. Your good-looking client might be looking for work. He just doesn't know it yet."

By mid-afternoon, Lana had cleared her desk and begun to daydream about how she wanted her little house to look. When Mack McClaren's tall figure passed her office's interior window, she was jolted out of her reverie. She clicked onto her daily planner and saw that the receptionist had scheduled him for a three o'clock appointment. She leaped to her feet and straightened her skirt. "Good afternoon, Mr. McClaren."

"I hope so," he said.

Lana glanced across her desk at him. If she'd had to guess, she would have said he looked troubled. She didn't think her news was going to help.

"Your application has been reviewed, Mr. McClaren."

"Mack," he corrected her.

"Sorry. Mack. Unfortunately, I can't put it through as we originally submitted it."

Mack sagged against the back of the chair and ran a hand through his dark curls. His eyes met hers and Lana continued, "However, I think we can still do something for you if you're willing to take a look at some options."

Mack pulled himself forward, more resigned than excited, Lana thought. He rested his elbows on the front of her desk and stared at the papers she slid toward him.

"Since the hotel project is not a sure thing, the bank suggests we start with an increase in your line of credit rather than an outright loan. If, and/or, when the hotel project develops we can review the situation at that time. How does that sound?"

Mack silently ran a blunt fingertip over the figures before him, shaking his head. Lana could read the disappointment in his features—the slump of his shoulders, the furrows on his brow. Finally, he heaved a sigh and sat back.

"If it's the best we can do," he said, looking at her, "I guess I'd better take it. I'm going to have to scale back on some of my plans though, which means putting some other projects on hold."

Lana had never run her own business but she knew enough about financing them to understand that not getting the funds Mack sought might mean he had to settle for less than he'd planned.

"I'm sorry we can't do more for you right now," she said. "but you must understand the bank's position, too. Now, let's get these papers signed and I'll get the line of credit increase active for you right away."

Ten minutes later, all the formalities had been completed. "Your credit line increase is now live, Mr. McClaren, I mean, Mack. You can use it any time you need to."

Mack flipped his cap back onto his head and stood up.

"Before you go," Lana said, "there's one more thing I would like to discuss with you."

Mack sat back down. "Yeah, what's that?"

"I just bought a house out on Sandpiper Road. It needs a lot of work and I'm looking for a contractor to help me with the renovations." Lana felt her heart ticking up a racing patter. She tried to ignore it. "Would you, um, be interested in taking a look at it?"

"What's the address?"

"3925 Sandpiper Road."

Mack nodded slowly, not taking his eyes off hers. "I know that house. Needs a lot of work."

Lana swallowed. "It does. I think it has potential, though. What do you think?"

"It depends whether the foundation is still sound and what kind of shape the structure is in but..." He shook his head. "...I couldn't say about the rest. I'd have to take a look at it."

"Will you?" Lana's voice squeaked and she cleared her throat to cover it up. "I have only two weeks until I have to move out of my current place. Is there any possibility you could come this afternoon, after I get off work?"

Mack tilted his head to one side. The way he looked at Lana made her want to squirm. It felt like he could see right through her. "Sure," he answered. "I guess I can do that. Why don't I meet you out there at what? Six?"

Lana expelled the breath she had been holding without realizing it.

"Yes, six. Thank-you. I'll bring us something to eat while we view the house."

"Deal." Mack stood, shook Lana's hand, and walked out the door.

Chapter Four

Rather than going straight back to her apartment after work, Lana stopped by Murphy's Mercantile to pick up some ready-made food for a makeshift dinner. She didn't want to give Mack any reason to rush away, such as, he was hungry. Lana knew feeding a man usually produced better work, so she bought pasta salad, ham and Swiss cheese croissants, black olives, and bottles of elderflower cordial.

"I'll take a half dozen of those double chocolate brownies," Lana said, indicating the state-of-the-art desserts in a glass case near the cash register in Murphy's. Each brownie was the size of the palm of her hand. *That should keep him energized*, she thought.

"Having a picnic?" Meghan Murphy, owner Liam Murphy's daughter, asked as she wrapped up the brownies.

"You could say that," Lana answered. "I'm trying to woo a contractor into renovating my house."

Meghan smiled. "That wouldn't be Mack McClaren, would it?"

"How did you know?"

She shrugged one shoulder. "Word gets around. Summersby Island isn't a very big place."

Lana nodded. "Got any inside tips for me?"

"He loves licorice, the salty Dutch stuff." She grabbed a little paper bag, flicked it open and scooped in a portion from a candy jar on top of the glass case. "This is like catnip. You'll have him eating out of your hand in a minute."

Lana grinned as she paid for the groceries and picked up the bag. "Thanks. I'll let you know how it turns out."

Mack's silver F350 pickup truck already stood in the driveway of Lana's newly acquired property when she arrived. She got out of the rental car she had taken for a month, leaving the food and treats inside—except, that is, for the licorice. She stuffed the little paper bag into her purse and walked toward the house. Mack was nowhere to be seen but before she reached the broken-down steps to the veranda, a furry black and white blur raced around the corner of the house and nearly knocked her off her feet. Lana made a wild grab for a splintery newel post. She was able to identify the speeding animal as a Border collie, the kind of dog used to herd sheep in Scotland. The dog made three circles around her then leapt off the veranda and disappeared around the side of the house. A second later he was back, tongue lolling as he skidded to a stop next to her right leg.

"Jasper, where did you go?" Lana heard Mack's voice calling from somewhere on the far side of the property. "We're supposed to be working here."

"He's over here with me," Lana called out. The dog sat down next to her foot and looked up at her. "Hello, Jasper." Lana crouched down to slide her hand over the smooth crown of his head.

Mack appeared around the corner of the house. "I see you've made a new friend," he said. "He doesn't usually take to strangers so this is a good endorsement of your character."

Lana smiled. "I'm relieved to hear it."

For a moment Mack watched Lana as she became acquainted with his usually standoffish dog. When Lana looked up at him, Mack said, "I nearly didn't come, you know."

Lana gave him a quizzical look.

"You're not exactly my favorite person right now. Because of the loan, I mean." A frown creased his brow but his eyes didn't leave hers.

"I want you to know I really went to bat for you at the bank. But the decision isn't mine alone. I haven't been working at the bank long and I guess I didn't have enough clout to carry it through."

Mack threw his hands up. "Then why did I end up with you and not with someone who could have made it happen?"

Lana straightened up, heat rising behind her ears. "It wouldn't have made a difference. The team decides and they decided against my recommendation. If you don't want to be here, please feel free to leave. I'm sure you're not the only building contractor on the island."

Mack reached up and flipped the cap off his head by the bill then gazed off past his left shoulder. "Actually," he said finally, "I probably am. Everybody else has gone over to the mainland to work on a new resort complex. I stayed here to finish up some other jobs and try to get things in order for the big hotel project. It looks like you're stuck with me."

"You mean you'll stay? You'll work on my house?"

"That's what I said. Let's get to it."

Lana nearly allowed her shoulders to slump with the wave of relief washing over her but caught herself and drew in a long breath instead. There was no point letting Mack know how elated she felt about him not turning around and walking away.

"I've had a look at the foundation from the outside already so if you've got the key we can go inside. The house is pretty run down, like nobody gave a hoot about its upkeep for a long time."

"Apparently, the man who lived here was quite old so he must have had difficulty with it," Lana said. She pulled the house key from a pocket on the side of her purse. "Then after he died, the family fought over the will for years, further neglecting the property. Can you imagine a family doing that?"

Mack raised his eyebrows. "Yeah, some families are their own worst enemies. Come on, let's see what we've got here."

By now, the interior of the house had grown dark so Lana found a light switch and flicked it. Nothing happened.

"Probably a burnt out bulb," Mack suggested. "But the wiring could be shot. These old houses…"

She stepped over some chipped plaster lying on the hallway floor and went into the living room where the light from the west windows slanted in. The place smelled as musty and dirty as it had when she and

Sherry explored it, and the odor was topped off with the faint tang of animal droppings. "It needs a good cleaning, that's for sure," Lana said.

Mack pulled a flashlight out of his back pocket and walked around the perimeter of the room, thumping on walls and examining floorboards. He shone the light beam around the area where the ceiling met the top of the walls.

"Walls seem sound," he said. "Let's look at the rest of the place."

Lana followed Mack as he examined the remainder of the house then shoved the sliding glass door open and went outside again. He gazed up at the veranda roof and kicked one of its uprights with the steel toe of his boot.

Lana was almost afraid to ask but took the plunge anyway. "So, can you do anything with it? I've already signed the papers."

Mack looked at her. "Ordinarily, I would say that was a pretty dumb thing to do but I happen to know how hard it is to get beach property on the island. It's a beautiful spot. I assume you got a good deal or we wouldn't be here."

Lana nodded but didn't elaborate. After all, she had an advantage over Mack when it came to getting a bank loan. "The bank wanted to get rid of the headache. They were happy to let it go. Is it worth fixing or did I just buy myself a dump that needs to have a can of gas and a match thrown on it?"

Mack gave her a cautious smile. "No need to go that far," he said. "Most of what it needs is cosmetic but we'll have to replace the roof, and the deck on the front is a threat to life and limb. We should see what's under that monstrosity of a carpet, too. It might need new floorboards as well."

"I know it's getting dark but if we could take a look now, it would save time. I have to move in here in two weeks. You're free to start work right away, aren't you?"

"As luck would have it, yes," Mack said. "Things kind of slowed down suddenly."

"Good. I mean, good for me, maybe not for you. I'm sorry."

"Don't be. I could use a smaller job right now. Once I get to work on the hotel project, there'll be no rest for the weary."

Lana led the way back through the kitchen to the living room.

"Hold on a second," Mack said. "I'll grab something from the truck to yank up the carpet."

In a minute he was back, and two minutes later he had the corner of the worn carpet free and ripped away from the walls. "Just as I suspected," he said. "It's bird's-eye maple. Nice stuff."

He shone the beam of the flashlight around the bared floor and even though dust and carpet fibres coated the wood, Lana could see that with some care and refinishing it could be beautiful.

Mack faced Lana. "I think we'd better sit down and figure out what you want done here. Then I can give you a price and you can decide how you want to proceed."

Chapter Five

"Ouch!" Lana cried as the nail file slipped out of the staple and sliced the side of her finger. Someone in the past had thought it a good idea to use a stapler to fasten drooping pieces of wallpaper back up on the bedroom walls.

Mack left whatever he was doing in the kitchen and appeared in the bedroom doorway. He leaned against the doorframe. "I think what you need here is a man." He hitched his thumbs into his jeans pockets and surveyed Lana's reddened finger.

"It seems to me," she replied, "that what I need in this case is a trip to a hardware store for a box of decent tools. Since you won't let me touch your precious collection, maybe you can help me get some of my own."

Mack pulled a clean handkerchief from his back pocket and dabbed at the drop of blood that had appeared on her skin. "I'll tell you what. While you're at work tomorrow, I'll pick up a few real tools for you so you don't have to remove petrified staples with your girly purse tools."

"Actually, I'd like to go with you. I'm no stranger to maintaining a place but I've never had a decent hammer in my life. Why don't we meet at the hardware store after I get off work tomorrow?"

"Have it your way." Mack stuffed the handkerchief back into his pocket and went back to work.

As Lana watched him leave the room her thoughts slid back to what had happened the previous evening.

After she and Mack had done a thorough assessment of the work the house required, Mack said, "We have to go over what it's going to take for all this. I'll get my stuff from the truck and be back in a minute."

"I'll come with you," Lana replied. "I have food in the car for us and a big beach towel. If it's all right with you, why don't we go out onto the beach? We can eat and get this official stuff done while we watch the sun go down."

Mack hesitated.

"What?" Suddenly wary, Lana wondered if he might decide to walk away after all. She dreaded the thought of having to find a contractor from the mainland and with the house's present condition, moving in without having the work done was unthinkable. She suppressed a shudder.

Mack shook his head. "Nothing."

Lana unrolled the big sea turtle beach towel she had bought almost the minute she arrived on Summersby Island. Murphy's Mercantile, which seemed to have at least a half dozen of just about everything, had recently received a huge order of beach towels in the most delicious island colors and designs the day after she arrived in town. Lana spent forty-five minutes trying to choose between the turquoise one with baby sea turtles all over it, and the bright green one covered with dancing pink flamingos. In the end, she gave up and bought them both—one for the house, and one to keep in the car for impromptu beach stops, or for company should she ever have any.

"Have a seat," she instructed Mack who still looked like he might break and run. "I've got croissants and elderflower drinks. Oh, and I have something else for you." She reached into her purse and pulled out the little paper bag of licorice and handed it up to him.

"What's this?"

"Open it."

The paper crackled as he stuck a finger into the sack. Then he peered in. "Who told you?"

Lana grinned. "I have my sources. Do you want to start with those or are you going to sit down and eat something good for you?" She peeled the lid off the pasta salad.

Mack settled on the sand at the opposite end of the towel. Lana handed him a paper plate piled high with everything she had bought earlier. He set it on the towel and pulled a pencil out of the folder he'd brought from the truck. "Here's a list of what I think the house needs. Some of it is optional so it's up to you if you want to do it now or later." He bit into the ham and Swiss croissant and scribbled on a yellow pad. "You'll want to rip up the carpeting and pull down the wallpaper."

"That's for sure," Lana agreed. "Can the floor underneath be refinished or will I have to buy new floor coverings?"

"Mm," Mack said. He swallowed. "It's beautiful wood. All it needs is sanding and sealing and you're good to go. You might want to put something like ceramic tiles in the kitchen and bathroom but it's up to you. The walls need sanding and painting or papering again if that's what you want. I can get the contractors for you for those jobs." He scribbled some more. "The deck on the street side of the house needs to be ripped right out and replaced. We can change the size or shape of it too, so now is the time to decide what you want and whether to put a full roof on it." Mack went on to list a host of other fixes, large and small, as Lana watched his sturdy hand move across the paper. She pulled the container of fudge brownies from the grocery bag and gulped with mounting alarm at the growing inventory of repair issues.

When Mack's pencil finally stopped, Lana peered at his notes. "How much will all that cost?"

Mack scribbled a number on the bottom of the pad and held it out toward her. By now, the sun was so low she had to squint to read it. "This is the best case scenario," Mack explained, "meaning if we do everything on the list. It'll be tight to get it all done in two weeks but we've pulled off a few miracles before."

Lana stared at the figure scribbled on the page. There was no way she could pay for all of this. She'd have to get a second job for the next ten years. She bit her bottom lip and frowned. Then she handed the pad back to him. "Start crossing off the unnecessary, all the things that can wait, and let's see where we end up."

"Why don't you tell me your budget, Lana? It will save us both a lot of time."

Lana made a quick mental calculation as Mack tipped the elderflower drink to his lips. When she named her figure, he choked on the drink, gasping and coughing, his eyes wet with tears. Her heart sank. Did this mean she would have to do the work herself? There was no way she could fix the rotting front porch, or put a new roof on the house. She could probably strip the old paper off the walls and paint them herself. She'd painted before when her mother had handed her a can of paint and a brush and headed out the door for her second job of the day. Lana had even become pretty good at it. But ripping up flooring and sanding the wood beneath it sounded like a monumental task and she would have to do it while living in the mess.

"Sorry," Mack said. "That went down the wrong way. Are you sure that's the best we can do?"

Lana liked how he used the term "we." Maybe there was still hope of having him do the work. "I can help," she answered. "I know how to do lots of things, and I take direction well. The problem is, I can only work at the house after I get off work at the bank, and on weekends. But there are only two weekends left in the month. Let's go over the list and you can tell me what jobs should be done first and what each will cost." She placed the remains of the sunset picnic into the shopping bag and slid closer to Mack. A light breeze from the northwest picked up and she caught the faint scent of his woodsy aftershave.

Half an hour later it was too dark to read outside but the two of them had sketched out a plan to get started on the house while Mack munched on chunk after chunk of licorice. He would begin the very next morning by stripping and refinishing the floors while a couple of his employees tackled the living room and bedroom walls. The woodwork around the doors and windows needed refinishing, as did the baseboards. The house had no dining room to speak of, only a corner in the kitchen for a table and a space at one end of the living room where another table could be squeezed in. That cut down on the number of rooms requiring work. Two small bedrooms and the minuscule bathroom competed the floor plan. Mack agreed to have his plumber friend, Phil, come by and check out the pipes and another tradesman, named Carlos, examine the wiring.

"Can't you tell if they need work?" Lana asked. She knew the more trades the renovation required, the more it would cost.

Mack shook his head. "I'd only be making an educated guess and you don't want that. Don't worry though; it won't take them long and they both owe me favors so it won't cost much."

Relieved, Lana nodded. "What will we do about the kitchen? It's nothing short of vile and I know rodents and birds have been living in there. There's no way I'm going to prepare food in that revolting place."

When it was too dark to see, they packed up their things and trekked back through the house. Now they stood near their vehicles. Jasper had already jumped into the cab of Mack's pickup and was curled up for a nap. "Leave that to me," Mack said. "I have a few connections so maybe we can get some deals. You'll want new appliances too, right?"

Lana's eyes widened. "Yes! Have you seen those monstrosities?"

Mack reached out and patted her shoulder. "Relax. We'll find you some new ones and they won't cost a fortune either, if you don't mind the odd scratch or ding."

A few minutes later, Lana backed out of the lane and followed Mack's taillights toward town. She could still feel a warm spot on her shoulder where his hand had touched her.

Chapter Six

"What is the matter with me, Jasper?" Mack turned the key his front door. His house, a narrow two-story that stood a block back from the beach, south of Summersby's town center, was dark and silent when he entered. Jasper raced past him and skidded on the polished wood floor as he headed for his supper dish.

"I can't do a job this cheaply," Mack muttered after he'd closed the door and flicked on the lights. Jasper sat watching Mack's hands as he opened a can of dog food and spooned the pink mixture into the waiting dish. "I'm going to lose money on this one, and why? Darned if I know. But Jas, doesn't she have the most gorgeous hair you've ever seen? All shiny and…that deep red." He sighed as Jasper polished off his meal in four gulps. "And those eyes…"

Lana had insisted Mack take the container of leftover brownies. He set it on the counter and stared out the window. "They're kind of blue and kind of green. I've never seen eyes that color before." He went through the motions of getting a small plate from the cupboard, placing the remaining brownies on it and sitting down at the table. Suddenly, his solitary life seemed to yawn before him like an echoing dark cavern. He imagined Lana sitting across from him, licking chocolate icing from her fingertips, as she had done only an hour ago on the beach.

Jasper wandered over and rested his muzzle on Mack's leg, as though sensing Mack's mood. Mack stroked the dog's smooth head and tousled the fur behind his ears. "I'm going to have to call in lots of favors for this job, buddy. I guess I'd better start phoning first thing in the morning."

Lana was out of bed and dressed before the morning sun had crept over the horizon. She slicked pink lipstick on, pressed her lips together then grabbed her steaming insulated coffee mug and headed for her car. If she hurried, she just had time to go past her house before her 8:00 a.m. meeting at the bank. She knew Sally wouldn't look favorably at a tardy entrance. She never did with anyone else.

The rising sun flickered through the palm fronds and flashed across her windshield as Lana rolled along the street that would soon be her address. She could hardly believe how fast everything had happened. She'd gone from the depth of disappointment at receiving yet another eviction notice, straight to the high of signing the papers on her own home. *My own home*, she thought with glee, hardly believing the sound of it. She slowed for a speed bump then crept along the street as she neared her house. She didn't really have a plan; she simply wanted to look at it to know it was real.

When Lana rounded the last curve before her lane she could see that the scrubby yard already held four work vehicles. "Oh, my goodness! He took me seriously." She had signed her name to Mack's quote, but for some reason still didn't quite trust that he would show up like he'd promised. She'd been let down by so many men before, she didn't believe any of them were entirely dependable. Her past was littered with tradesmen, mechanics, repairmen, and security men—the kind of men who were supposed to be trustworthy but had proven otherwise. And the ones who had promised to be true, like her father and her recently-departed boyfriend—departed for the

Caribbean, that is—had also let her down. So to see Mack's pickup truck parked in her driveway along with an electrician's van and a plumber's van was a shock.

A bubble of happiness trickled upward from somewhere in Lana's belly and erupted in a smile she could not hold back. She glanced at the clock on the dashboard, then eased her foot down on the accelerator and spun the wheel back toward town.

"What are you grinning about?" Sherry said as she and Lana refilled their coffee cups in the bank's tiny kitchen. "You looked like the cat that swallowed the canary all through the meeting."

"I went by my house this morning."

"And?"

"The yard was full of work trucks."

Sherry raised one eyebrow. "And this is news because…"

"Mack McClaren is renovating my house. Don't you see? He actually showed up, with plumbers and electricians and everything."

"You hired him, didn't you?" Sherry stirred two sugars into her coffee mug. "What did you expect him to do?"

"Sher, you don't get it. I don't think I've met a man yet who didn't turn out to be a disappointment, or who lied to me, or who didn't keep his promises. From the day my dad walked out when I was five, to Carl most recently, you could say I've had a string of bad luck when it comes to men. To have a guy say he'll do something then actually do it, well, it might not seem like much to you but it means a lot to me."

Sherry laid her spoon in the sink and placed both hands on Lana's shoulders. "Honey, you need to get a new image of men. They're not all weasels and skunks, you know. Mack McClaren is a good guy. I've never known him not to keep his word. I think that's why he was so devastated when Shayla walked out on their wedding day. In his world that's something you simply don't do."

"Hey, you two." Owen Sheffield's voice interrupted the two women. "Can a guy get in here and pour himself a coffee?"

"Just leaving," Lana said. "It's all yours."

By five o'clock, Lana felt more than ready to leave the office. She'd had appointments and paperwork all day but could hardly keep her mind on her work. The prospect of meeting Mack again had her as nervous as a mosquito in a repellent factory. She switched off her office lights and closed the door.

"Going home to pack tonight?" Sherry fell into step beside Lana. "Or are you shopping for paint colors?"

Lana quickened her pace. "I have an appointment with my contractor to pick out some tools over at the hardware store."

"Tools, huh? Whatcha gonna do with those?" Sherry teased.

Lana glanced at her. "I'm renovating a house, remember? I need some decent tools so I can do some of the work. It's the only way I can save money on the project. Besides, we have so little time, all hands have to be on deck."

"Sure you do." Sherry laughed as she turned toward her car. "Have fun with those tools." She gave Lana a little wave over her shoulder. Lana frowned and went in the other direction.

When Lana pushed open the door to Murphy's Mercantile, the place was nearly deserted, except for a woman with a small boy who walked out the door as Lana entered. Meghan stood near the sidewall holding an armload of bright garments.

There was no sign of Mack.

"Hey, Lana," Meghan called out. "What can I do for you?"

Lana wandered over to where Meghan was unloading a big box of children's swimsuits and hanging them on pegs.

"I'm supposed to meet Mack McClaren here about some tools but I don't see him yet."

"In that case, do you mind watching the store for a minute? I haven't been to the ladies' room for hours and Dad's out back fixing a mower. I won't be long."

"Sure, no problem," Lana answered. Meghan raced off toward the rear of the building.

Brightly-colored, stretchy little suits lined the wall in front of Lana, some of them sized for newborns. *Do newborns need bathing suits?* Lana wondered. She had no idea what babies wore but she couldn't resist reaching out to touch the hot pink ruffles of a tiny suit. On shelves below the suits, tiny flip flop sandals were lined up like crayons in a box, in every color and style, from neon green to zebra print. Lana sighed as she picked up a pair of yellow sandals no more than three inches from toe to heel. Would she ever have her own little girl to dress in adorable things like this, she wondered? Probably not, given her romance history.

"Pretty cute, aren't they?"

Lana had been so lost in thought she hadn't heard Mack come in. She jumped at the sound of his voice then placed the baby shoes back on the shelf.

"Yeah, they are," she agreed.

"Have you got somebody to buy those for?" he asked casually.

She shook her head. "No one at all."

"That's kind of a shame. Little kids are a lot of fun. They're work, but they're fun, too."

"How do you know?" Lana faced him.

"Nieces and nephews. I have a big family."

"Then you should be the one buying things like this," Lana said.

"Their parents can do that," Mack told her. "Let's go look at the tools."

Meghan reappeared. "Thanks for helping out, Lana. You guys know where all the tools are, don't you? Shout if you need anything and I'll keep working on this new stock."

It took Mack less than fifteen minutes to outfit Lana with a tool belt, hammer, tape measure, cordless drill, and a sharp cutter.

"If you need anything else, you can borrow mine," he said. He tightened the tool belt around her hips. She held her breath as he leaned near her. "There, that should work for you." He checked out the fit by tugging on the band of the belt. Lana felt like he had plugged her into an electric socket.

"I thought you didn't lend your tools," she said.

"Ordinarily, I don't." He grinned. "But, well…I might make an exception this time."

The Summersby Island House

Chapter Seven

As they left the store, Lana told Mack she planned to go back to her apartment, change into jeans and a t-shirt and head over to the house. "What can I work on there tonight?" she asked.

"You can't go in the house tonight," Mack informed her. "We refinished the floors today and the sealant isn't dry enough to walk on yet. You could give me a hand ripping the boards off that rotting deck, though—if you feel up to it."

"Haven't you been at the house all day? You don't have to work this evening, too."

Mack shrugged. "I don't have anything else pressing to do and I know you're on a tight timeline." Just knowing Lana planned to be at the house this evening was a good enough reason for him to go back to work. His subcontractors had all gone home, which made it all the better. The two of them would be alone.

"Well, thank-you," Lana said. "What if I pick up some food so we can eat something before we start? I'll meet you there in about forty-five minutes."

Almost on the minute, Lana pulled her car up beside Mack's truck and hopped out. She'd rushed home, changed clothes, made fresh strawberry lemonade, ordered pizza, packed plates, cutlery and glasses, picked up the pizza, and driven to the house. Mack set down his pry bar and sat down on the edge of what was left of the deck. The old railing and spindles lay in a pile on the ground.

Mack lifted the lid of the pizza box. "What kind did you get?"

Lana poured some drinks. "Double anchovy, Greek," she replied.

Mack glanced in her direction. "Uh, great! My favorite."

"It is not," Lana said, laughing. "I got ham and pineapple on one half, and pepperoni on the other. I was testing you."

Mack's lips curved up in a grin. "Did I pass?"

"Oh, yes. You get a check mark in the 'easy to get along with' category." She dished up a wedge of pizza and handed the plate to him.

"You have a checklist? With categories?" His brow furrowed.

"Sure. So do you. Yours probably has things like good-looking, nice, can cook, knows which end of a hammer to hold, right? In spite of appearances to the contrary," Lana added, "I can cook. I had to learn early."

"Good to know," Mack said through a mouthful of cheesy ham and pineapple. "Why did you have to learn early?"

"Single mom who was always working—long story."

For a few minutes Mack didn't respond. "So, what's on your checklist anyway?"

Lana liked the way his left eyebrow dipped when he looked worried. His eyes flicked in her direction.

"Knows which end of the hammer to hold," she replied with a grin. "And that's all I'm telling you."

"We'll see about that," Mack said. "I have ways of finding out things."

They worked together, ripping the old planks from the deck's frame and then, once they saw the condition of the frame, tearing it out as well. By the time it was too dark to work, they were both exhausted.

The next day Lana packed her work clothes in a duffle and threw it in the trunk of the rental car so she wouldn't have to waste time going back to her apartment to change. When she drove up to the house, she saw Mack had completed the entire new deck during the day, minus the roof. Already the house looked ten times better. She could see the glass installer working on one of the street side windows and when she poked her head in the front door she saw drop cloths spread on the floors. The painters had already started on the living room.

She found Mack in the smaller of the two bedrooms prying baseboards from the walls.

"Hey," she said. He turned toward her and smiled and her heart did a little flip-flop. Those killer dark eyes, with their rim of long black lashes, were doing a number on her. She drew in a quick breath. "How's it going in here?"

"Great. Want to give me a hand stripping this wallpaper? Glen and the gang want to sand and paint in here tomorrow."

"Sure. Now that I have proper tools and don't have to use my 'girly purse tools' it should be a snap."

They worked shoulder to shoulder prying out staples and peeling off layers of yellowed wallpaper.

Lana felt enveloped in Mack's scent—woodsy, musky, all male—that made her insides feel all syrupy.

Mack spread a tarp on the floor to collect all the debris and as he gathered it up to haul outside, his arm brushed against Lana's. Electricity traveled from her wrist to her shoulder, making her light-headed.

"Uh, sorry," Mack said. "Let me get this stuff out of our way, then we need to make some decisions about the kitchen."

All Lana could manage to do was nod. She wasn't at all sorry.

"This kitchen is a horror," Lana said once Mack joined her there. His nearness in the small room made her pulse pound but there was no way she wanted him to know that. She had already decided one heartbreak per winter was her limit. "Can we tear out the cabinets and put in all new ones?"

Mack rubbed his earlobe, something he did, Lana had noticed, when stalling. "Your budget doesn't allow for new cabinets. Sometimes you can get used ones, but usually you wouldn't want them anyway. I'm sure these could be cleaned up and painted so they're serviceable enough to last until you can redo the whole room. What do you think?"

Lana's heart sank but she pasted on a tiny smile. She'd lived in so many two-bit, rundown apartments and ramshackle houses while growing up, with tacky kitchens and sticky cracked linoleum, the thought of having to make do with yet another one almost nauseated her. She sighed and straightened her shoulders anyway. She looked around. "I'm sure I can do something with this room. A little paint, a rug on the floor, some pretty curtains..."

"I'll give you a hand wherever I can," Mack said. He reached out and stroked her shoulder. "Why don't we make a list of what you'll need to shop for? Things like new hinges and drawer pulls are inexpensive and they're easy to install. That will make a world of difference." He went on to name several supplies she would need to spruce up the dismal room. His solicitous manner and creative ideas buoyed her and by the time she'd written down everything he suggested she felt almost enthusiastic. Almost, but not quite.

"I still have to buy new appliances," Lana reminded him. "There is no way I'm using these, even if they do work, which I seriously doubt. So I have to figure that into my budget, too."

"I'll tell you what," Mack said, "we've been working hard here all week. Why don't I take you out for dinner tomorrow night instead of coming over here? Then on Saturday we can head over to the mainland. I've got some good connections with a couple of appliance dealers. I'm pretty sure I can swing a better deal on a fridge and stove than you could get by yourself. What do you say?"

Is he asking me out on a date? This could change the dynamic of their relationship. Until now he was simply the guy who was working for her. She bit the inside of her lower lip, a habit she had when she needed to think hard and fast.

Mack gave her forearm a shake. "Hey, it's only dinner, not a G12 Summit. We both have to eat anyway, so why not go together? I'll even pay. I've got a great line of credit and we can talk about the house while we eat, so I can write off the expense. Same goes for the trip on Saturday. I need a few other supplies anyway. We might as well kill two birds with one stone, right?"

Lana couldn't help but laugh. "Since you put it like that, all right."

The Summersby Island House

Chapter Eight

The first ferry on Saturday morning left at 8:00 a.m. and at 8:07 Lana stood at the railing on the upper deck next to Mack, sipping a cup of bitter coffee from a vending machine. The trip took only twenty minutes start to finish so there was barely time to leave the vehicle before they had to get back down below and be ready to drive off.

"It's another pretty day out here," Mack said.

Lana nodded even though a brisk cool wind penetrated her sweater. A pair of gulls wheeled overhead, searching for free snacks. Lana drew her sweater closer and hugged it to her middle.

"Are you cold?" Mack asked. "Here, take my jacket." He slipped it over Lana's shoulders, allowing his arm to linger across her back as he rubbed her opposite arm. Her heart rate ticked up a few notches as Mack pulled her toward his warm body. It lasted only a moment but felt better than she could have imagined.

Once off the ferry, Mack drove his pickup truck to the nearest appliance dealer he knew.

"Hey, Jerry," Mack said. He reached to shake hands with the salesman who had sprinted toward the door when he and Lana entered the store. "How's it going?"

"Mack, it's great to see you again. It's been ages."

Mack introduced Lana and Jerry. Jerry was the same height as Lana and had thinning brown hair and pale blue eyes behind horn-rimmed glasses.

Mack explained the purpose of their shopping trip, then Jerry gave Lana his pitch for the most expensive appliances in the store, leading her from one fabulous fridge and stove to the next. Finally, Mack stopped him. "Jerry, you have to do better than this. Come here, I need to talk to you in private." Mack excused himself to Lana and drew Jerry aside behind some shelves. A couple of minutes later, they came back.

"Listen, Lana," Jerry said. "Mack's an old friend so let me show you something I'm sure you're going to like." The appliances he demonstrated now were much more in line with both the space available in

Lana's tiny kitchen and with the price she was prepared to pay.

After a little negotiating, Jerry came down even more in price. Lana smiled sweetly at him. "Could you put that in writing please and sign it? I'd like to look around a bit more before making my decision." Jerry agreed and Lana and Mack got back in the truck.

"What did you say to him back there?" Lana asked. She fastened her seatbelt. "He sure changed his tune fast."

Mack's eyebrow came down over his right eye and she could see the corner of his mouth squeeze into a grin. "I told him I'm trying to impress you by getting a good deal and he wasn't helping."

Lana's head snapped toward him. "You did not!"

He shrugged then pulled out into the traffic heading east. "It worked, didn't it?"

After two more stops, including a quick lunch at a downtown coffee shop, they ended up back at the same appliance store where they had started. The evening before, when Mack had taken Lana out for dinner at Sabra's On The Island, the only restaurant on Summersby that served Greek food, she had mentioned her rental car had to go back to the depot in a few days and she had to start looking for a bicycle to get around town.

Before going back into the appliance store, Mack asked, "Say, do you want to look for a bike while we're here."

She batted her eyelashes at him deliberately. "What? You mean Jerry sells bikes too?"

"No, Betty Boop. I mean here in Sarasota."

Lana laughed. "I knew what you meant. I think I'd rather just order the appliances and go home. It's been a long and tiring week."

"Good call," Mack agreed. "But we don't have to order and wait for the appliances. They have both the fridge and stove in stock and we can load them into the pickup. That way you won't have to pay shipping and delivery. Believe me, that can add a bundle when you're talking about bringing things out to the island."

Soon Lana's new refrigerator and stove were loaded into Mack's truck. By the time Mack and Lana arrived back on the ferry, the sun was listing toward the horizon. They left the truck only long enough to get a drink from the vending machine and sit for a few minutes to watch the dolphins racing alongside the ferry before getting back in the vehicle and waiting for it to dock on Summersby Island. Mack had arranged for a couple of friends to meet them at Lana's house to unload the appliances.

After Seth and Andrew had helped lug the heavy appliances into the kitchen, they took off, leaving Mack and Lana alone in the waning light coming through the sliding patio doors overlooking the beach.

"I can't thank you enough for everything you've done for me today," Lana said. "I'm sure I'd never have gotten the kind of deal on these appliances without you. Did you really tell Jerry you were trying to impress me?"

Mack tilted his head to one side and smiled. "Maybe. Have I?"

Lana smiled back at him, holding his gaze. She nodded. "I'll say you have. You've been pretty amazing for a guy who hardly knows me."

"That last part is something we'll have to change then. I'll take 'amazing,' though." He reached toward her and gently took her elbow. "Come on, I'll drive you home. I think we're both done for the day."

On Sunday morning, Lana rose early and went for a walk on the beach. As she passed her house, she was tempted to go in and start working but instead she went back to her apartment, showered and dressed for church. The little chapel she had rediscovered when she returned to Summersby Island still stood where it had for the past eighty years. A new pastor had arrived the year before and, with enthusiastic fund-raising from the small congregation, the building had been spruced up inside and received a new coat of paint outside. The white clapboard exterior glowed in the morning sun as Lana mounted the front steps and greeted the Pastor, Dave.

After church, Lana went straight to her apartment and changed clothes, stopping just long enough to fix a sandwich before she headed to the house.

Sandpiper Road lay quiet under the noon sunshine. Lana parked the rental car and looked at the yard. *I'll have to start cleaning up all this debris.* If she did it before taking the car back, she could use the trunk to haul stuff away. *It will be a lot harder to do with a bicycle*, she thought ruefully. She would have to remember to ask Sherry about getting a bike here on the island. But for now, her attention focused on getting her house's kitchen in order.

She walked through the house, gazing at the changes that had taken place in the past week. The hardwood floors in the living room and bedrooms glowed gold under new shiny finishing. The electricity and plumbing had been updated, at least as much as they could be without tearing down the house and starting over. The walls boasted new paint in butter-soft colors. She moved through the kitchen, turning a blind eye to all the work it still required, and went out to the back patio and sat down on its edge. She pulled a décor magazine from her purse while she opened the wrapping on her sandwich.

Kicking off her sandals, she poked her feet out into the sun to warm up and flipped through the magazine as she ate. Mid-bite, she stopped and stared. On the page before her was the exact look she wanted for her own kitchen—pale tile floors, glossy white country cabinets, a new white sink, and a bump-out window over the sink with pots of herbs on the shelf. The backsplash, countertops, and wall colors reflected the sea before her with aqua, sand, sky blue, and white. She stared at the photos and read the descriptions in the sidebars. She loved the entire look, but it would have to wait. She didn't know how long she would have to endure the ghastly room as it stood now but there was no point stewing about it either. She crumpled the sandwich wrapper and stood up.

Once inside the house, she opened the magazine to her dream kitchen and laid it on the counter, then strapped on her new tool belt and pulled out the retractable cutter. The appliances had to be removed from their heavy packaging so she set to work slicing strapping and ripping off the cardboard. Before she could try to push them into place, that horrible floor had to be cleaned. How she would love to get rid of the grubby cracked linoleum! The longer she stared at the hopelessness of ever making the floor look good, the more determined she became that it had to go.

"I'll start with the cupboards and think about the floor later," she muttered as she filled a pail with hot, soapy water. She climbed up the stepladder Mack had left and started on the tops of the upper cabinets. Within a couple of swipes, she heard something rustle as her washrag swept the surfaces she couldn't see. Lana stood on tiptoe, reached up and pulled down crumpled sheet of paper. She dropped her rag into the pail and smoothed out the yellowed paper. On it was a child's drawing, a little stick girl holding the hand of a larger female figure with coiled yellow hair. The message read, *I love you Mommy. Sandra.* Arrows pointed to the characters showing the tall one as "Mommy" and the smaller figure as "Me."

Lana climbed down from the ladder, sank to the filthy linoleum on the floor, and burst into tears.

Chapter Nine

That's where Mack found her five minutes later.

"Hey," he said softly, squatting down beside Lana. "What's happened? Did you hurt yourself?"

Lana sniffed loudly and wiped the tears from her cheeks with a piece of paper towel. She handed Mack the dusty sheet of paper. He scanned it, his brow furrowing.

"Uh, is this someone you know?"

Lana shook her head and sniffed again.

Mack sat down on the floor beside her and encircled her in his arms. "Come here." He gently pulled her toward him and settled her head on his shoulder. "Want to tell me what this is about?"

After a few minutes, her final sniffle ended in a sigh. She sat up and took Mack's hand in both of hers. "Thank you for being so nice," she said. "I don't know why I had such a meltdown. There was something about that child's printing and the Mommy..." she drifted off.

"Come on, get up. Let's go for a little walk on the beach. You'll feel better." Mack took the yellowed paper and set it on the counter behind him and pulled Lana to her feet. He led her out through the sliding doors then took her hand as they walked across the sparkling sand toward the water's edge. Lana slipped off her sandals and stepped into the ripples kissing the shoreline.

"I don't want to pry but, what happened back there? Is the pressure getting to you?"

Lana scuffed the sand with her toes. "I guess it must be," she answered. "In only a few days I have to be out of my apartment. I don't even have furniture yet. Sherry, at work, has some things I can have and I've ordered a new bed from Mortinsen's Furniture downtown."

They walked in silence for a few more minutes, and then Mack said, "That's not it, is it? That's not what you were crying about."

Lana stopped walking. "No, it's not. I was thinking about that little girl who loved her mommy. My mommy died last year. She was only fifty-six."

"I'm so sorry, Lana. She was so young. What happened?"

"She had a heart problem no one knew about. Apparently, it was like a ticking time bomb. Personally, I think she finally died of exhaustion and a broken heart."

"Why do you say that?"

A puff of wind lifted a dark curl over Mack's ear. Lana resisted the urge to tuck it out of the way. "My dad walked out on us when I was five. Life was difficult. Mom often worked two or three jobs just to keep food on the table. We moved from place to place so I never knew any other family. No grandparents, no cousins, no siblings, no dad. All I've ever wanted is a real family, and when I read that note from a little girl named Sandra telling her mother she loved her, I guess I was blindsided. All those feelings came rushing back. For a while, well, there was this guy in Chicago…I thought it was pretty serious until I got laid off from my job. Then he dropped me like I had a disease. There's only me, all alone, now." She looked at Mack's profile, his strong jaw and straight nose and lips that always seemed to be ready to curve into a smile. She suddenly felt embarrassed that she'd said so much—embarrassed, and ashamed. "But, never mind," she said, spinning back toward the house. "I'm sure you don't want to hear all about my problems. Come on, I have a kitchen to scrub."

Mack's hand shot out and grasped her arm, turning her back toward him. "You're wrong, Lana. I do want to know. I want to know your whole story and if I can help at all, I want to do whatever I can."

"You're sweet," Lana said. But she didn't believe him for a moment.

Mack attempted to lighten Lana's mood. "Hey, you'll probably have a little girl or boy of your own one of these days who'll write you notes like that one you found."

Lana turned away from him and started walking. "I doubt it."

Mack caught up and reached for her hand, stopping her. "Why would you say that?"

"It's just not likely to happen for me, that's all." She headed up the beach toward the house. "I have to get this cleaning done and hook up the fridge and stove. Don't feel you have to stay and help." Then she stopped again. "By the way, what are you doing at my house on Sunday afternoon anyway?"

Mack shrugged. "I had nothing better to do so I thought I'd pound a few nails on the deck. I didn't want any accidents to happen."

"I see. Where's Jasper?"

"He didn't want to come."

"He didn't want to come? Your dog has opinions?"

"Oh gosh, yes. He was in a mood because I wouldn't let him run around town on his own last night. He's got a crush on the poodle down the street but her owner is determined to keep the lovers apart. He's been sulking ever since."

"Poor Jasper."

Mack walked with Lana back to the house and through the glass doors into the kitchen. "Hey, what's this?" he asked when he spied the magazine lying open on the countertop next to the sink. "Nice design."

Lana picked up her washrag and glanced his way. "It's what you call a dream," she said. "Someday, I want this kitchen to look like that one, but it won't be happening any time soon. Once the deck is done, and the roof, and the siding painted, and the bathroom updated so it doesn't make me want to cover my eyes every time I go in there, well, there won't be money to fix up the kitchen for a good long while. Never mind." She climbed up the stepladder and leaned into it, scrubbing the top shelves of the cabinets. "I can make do with this kitchen the way it is."

"Hmm," Mack said. "Well, I'd better hit the deck, or before I know it the day will be over and I won't have pounded a single nail. Get it? Hit the deck?" His hand circled her ankle and he gave it a squeeze. Lana felt an electric charge scamper up her calf.

"Very funny." She took a swat at his arm with the rag. "But if you knock me off this ladder, I won't get much done either."

Mack's touch gentled. "Feeling better now? No more tears?"

Lana looked into his upturned face. "I don't know what came over me. The thought of some mother living in this house with her own little girl who loved her…"

"It's not too late for you, Lana. Believe me, things can change."

She shook her head. "I'm tired of hoping. It's too painful. I just need to get on with it." She took a deep breath. "Starting with this filthy cupboard."

"Okay, I can take a hint," Mack said. "I'll let you know when I'm finished what I came to do. If you're up for it, maybe we could go out for a coffee later."

"Maybe," Lana replied absently as she tugged at a sticky fragment of burnt orange shelf liner.

Lana's appointment log for Monday had names in every schedule slot, names she didn't recognize, names of people she hoped would borrow money. She tried to be altruistic about the job she was doing and succeeded most of the time. The Carsons obtained a car loan the previous week. She had seen them driving their old car and felt gratified to be a part of their successful replacement of the dented 1989 Chevy Cavalier. She helped a retired couple from chilly Minnesota acquire the mortgage on a sweet little condo where they could escape those brutal winters for the first time in their lives. Marion Schwartz borrowed two thousand dollars to buy a better piano for her ultra-talented daughters to continue with classical music lessons, and Garry Wannamaker got a loan to buy a new boat to take visitors out fishing.

Helping all these people achieve their dreams gave Lana a great deal of pleasure but it also brought her relief. Having this much business now coming across her desk, her job security grew and with a mortgage now herself, that was pretty important to her.

Over sandwiches from the Mercantile on Tuesday, Lana and Sherry sat in Sherry's office and discussed curtain colors, what to do with the yard around Lana's house, and the fact that Lana's rental car was due back at the agency on the mainland in two days.

"I have to find something to get around the island but I'm in no position to buy a vehicle right now, not with all the renovation costs for the house," Lana told her friend. "It's too far from the house to walk to work in the morning, too, and Summersby has no bus service at all."

"Why don't you go see Larry Watson over at Pedal and Paddle? He might have some bikes you could look at. Either that or a kayak," Sherry said with a smirk. "You could hop in it over on your beach, paddle around the north end of the island, and dock it in the marina while you're at work."

Lana could see Sherry was biting the inside of her bottom lip to keep from laughing. "Oh, sure, I'll just hop out of it in my little business suit with tight skirt and heels and totter up the dock and into town every morning. What will I do if the wind is blowing?"

"Well," said Sherry, "then you paddle around the south end of the island so you don't get blown out to sea, and you hang onto your skirt when you totter up the dock."

"Ha ha," Lana replied, dryly. "Get serious. I need a set of wheels."

"Go talk to Larry, girlfriend. That guy has more deals up his sleeve than he has arm hairs."

"There's an image I don't want to see."

"He'll find you something you can ride."

"All right, I'll go after work today then I have to get over to the house again. I ordered bedding from Murphy's so I have to stop by there while I still have the car and pick it up as well as a heap of stuff for outfitting the kitchen. That's the trouble with moving to a new town with only the clothes on your back. I have to start over with everything."

"Listen," Sherry said. She sat up straighter and pushed her leftover sandwich aside. "I know you're busy like crazy trying to make the place liveable so you can get settled by the weekend, but once you're in there, let's have a party. It can be a combination house-warming slash shower party. I'll invite everyone you know and everyone I know and tell them all to bring presents for the house. You put on the food and drinks."

"You'd do that?"

"Sure, why not? Everybody's looking for something to do around here in February. It'll be fun."

Chapter Ten

Larry Watson's Pedal and Paddle Shop stood on a side street about three blocks from the bank. When Lana got off work, instead of going straight to the house, she popped back to her apartment and changed into a pair of navy leggings, white t-shirt, and a dark pink hoodie, all the while eating the first thing she saw in the refrigerator—leftover quiche. She slipped her feet into a pair of leather topsiders, jumped back into the car, and drove to the bike shop.

The front of the store, which was painted in candy colors of yellow, pink, and turquoise, had a big sign out front proclaiming that all kayaks were thirty percent off. Since it was almost March and the wintering tourists would be migrating back north soon, Lana realized the owner had to be anxious to grab the last of the winter business while getting it was still good.

A bell over the door tinkled as she went in. The

small store was deserted. Rows of bicycles crammed every inch of floor space. A couple of kayaks hung from the rafters, their glossy finishes glinting in the reflected sunlight coming through the plate glass windows. Lana could see a doorway at the rear of the room and through it more kayaks and what looked like a workshop with bike parts strewn about. She glanced around at some of the bicycles. She hadn't owned a bike since elementary school days, and even then it had been second, third, or fourth hand and invariably had a chain that perpetually jumped off the sprocket. She hardly knew what to look for but realized she wouldn't be buying a car any time soon so another mode of transportation had to be acquired. A bike was about the only thing in her price range, but when she lifted a tag and checked the price of a sleek lime green model with tires the diameter of a garden hose, she felt the blood drain from her face. If this was what bikes cost these days, she might have to settle for a good sturdy pair of walking shoes.

At that moment, a man emerged from the back room, wiping his hands on a greasy rag. He was tall and athletic-looking with sun-streaked blonde hair. The blue of his eyes very nearly matched the paint color on the front of the store.

"Hey," he said. He tossed the rag over his shoulder. It landed on a pair of handlebars. "Sorry I didn't hear you come in. I'm Larry. What can I do for you?"

Lana introduced herself and explained her transportation predicament.

"Do you consider yourself a cyclist, or do you want to become one?" Larry asked.

"Um, no, not really," Lana admitted, "but I need a way to get from my house out on Sandpiper Road to work downtown here. I won't have a car after tomorrow."

Larry asked a few more questions. "Do you plan to bike to work in your fancy bank duds? Skirt, heels, and all that?"

"Not if I don't have to," Lana admitted. "I suppose I can always change when I get there."

"Well, I don't want to decide for you but there's another option that might interest you. Follow me and I'll show you what I mean." Larry led the way into the back room, which was surprisingly spacious even though filled with kayaks, paddles, life vests, bike wheels and tires, odds and ends of bicycle parts, and even a couple of tiny pink tricycles. "It's over here. I don't normally carry these things, but a guy brought it in a few days ago and was desperate to sell before he left the island. Some family emergency or something."

Larry stopped before a shiny, powder blue, motorized scooter.

"Is that a Vespa?" Lana asked.

"Yeah, it's vintage but it's in perfect condition. Whoever owned it treated the thing like a baby. I've had a good look at it and have taken it out for a couple of spins after I closed the shop in the evening. It runs great."

Lana circled the machine. "It looks brand new."

"I checked and it's a 1973 model. Like I said, I don't normally sell motorbikes so I'd kind of like to get rid of it if I can get a decent price. Are you interested? You could ride it in a skirt and high heels if you had to,—if your skirt wasn't too, you know, flyaway—if you know what I mean."

Lana glanced his way and saw a blush bloom beneath his tan. "Oh, I know what you mean. But I've never ridden anything like this." She touched the handlebar. "Could I take it out for a ride?"

"Um, sure," Larry answered. "You're supposed to have a license but I doubt anyone's going to be patrolling this street if you just wanted to go down the block."

They discussed the price briefly but Lana remained non-committal. Given that he'd already told her he wanted the bike out of his shop, she felt sure she could talk him down a bit more, if she decided she liked it. Larry rolled the bike out onto the street and gave Lana a short course in how to start it, change gears, and use the accelerator and brakes. After ten minutes tootling up and down Corsair Street, Lana had fallen in love with the aged Vespa. Five minutes later, she had shaken hands with Larry and agreed to pick it up the following day.

"Hey, I can't interest you in a kayak, can I?" Larry asked as Lana headed for the front door. "They're on sale, thirty percent off."

She shook her head, smiled, and waved good-bye.

When Lana pulled her car into the driveway of her new house, all she could do was sit and stare. Mack and his crew had completely finished the deck on what she had begun to call the "sunrise side of the house," since it faced east. Not only that, but the rotting roof had been replaced with a sea-blue metal one that gleamed in the lowering sun. Mack had recommended replacing the siding rather than scraping and painting the decades-old wood that the house came with and now new white siding covered at least two sides of the building. *He has been busy*, she thought, grinning with glee. With her eviction day drawing ever closer, the days she spent working on the house had grown longer, and evidently so had Mack's. She had no idea whether this was normal behavior for builders and renovators but Mack kept assuring her that he'd get everything done on time, no matter what.

In the remaining five days before her move, which really only required that she pack her suitcases and throw her new towels into a shopping bag, she still had plenty to do.

As soon as Lana stepped out of her car, Sherry pulled in beside her and got out of her car, too. "I had to see the progress myself. Want to show me around?"

"I'd love to." Mack was nowhere in sight and Lana couldn't hear the sounds of power tools. The street was quiet except for a few keening gulls circling overhead. Once inside, Sherry stopped at the entrance to the living room.

"It's amazing," she said. "You'd hardly know it was the same house. And all this in what—ten days?"

Lana nodded. "It's starting to look liveable, which is a good thing because I have to move in here in less than a week. Let me show you the rest." The two women wandered through the bedrooms, checked out the bathroom that still needed work, and ended up in the kitchen. The last time Lana had worked in it she'd managed to wash down all the cabinets. Now the doors stood open, as she had left them to dry before painting.

Sherry looked around. "I see Mack hasn't gotten this far," she said.

"Grim, isn't it? This room is going to have to wait a while. I'm getting ready to paint everything and I've bought new hinges and handles, so that will perk it up a bit. I still shudder when I think of the vermin that made this room home before I got it. I scrubbed and disinfected until my arm nearly fell off and this is as good as it gets. Fridge and stove are new, though, but the rest of the house is in dire need of furnishing."

"What's this?" Sherry picked up the magazine from the counter. It was still open to the pages with Lana's dream kitchen.

"Oh, that's a fantasy I've been entertaining while I do the grunt work in here."

"Pretty," Sherry said. She dropped the magazine back onto the counter. "It would look nice in this house."

"That's what you call 'someday-country,'" Lana said. She closed the book.

"You need to talk to Mia at Mango Décor. Her shop is over on Parrot Crescent. Have you been in there yet?" Sherry grabbed Lana's arm and gave it a shake. "It is just the most gorgeous store south of Alaska."

"That's quite an endorsement. Does she sell tables and bedroom furniture? Right now, the boxes the fridge and stove came in are starting to look good."

"She's closed this evening, but tomorrow after work you and I are going shopping," Sherry informed her. "Now, let's start planning your house-warming shower."

Chapter Eleven

Lana didn't know how she could have missed Mango Décor and Gift. It was only four blocks from the bank where she worked. *Probably has something to do with the fact that I've done nothing but work and renovate a house since I landed on the island*, she thought. It was Friday night and Mango, as everyone evidently called the store, was open until 9:00 p.m.

Sherry introduced Lana to Mia, a petite woman in her late twenties, with spiky black hair and dark eyes. "Half Korean," Mia whispered, when Lana commented on her exotic looks. She offered Sherry and Lana glasses of White Zinfandel. "How can I help you tonight?"

"She needs everything," Sherry declared. "She has an empty house except for one bed and a couple of appliances. We're going to throw a house shower in a couple of weeks but the poor girl needs lamps, side tables, mirrors, rugs—you name it."

For the next hour and a half, Mia showed Lana everything in her store that was on Lana's list of needs. After a while Lana felt so confused, she couldn't make even the simplest decisions.

"I'll tell you what," Mia said. "Tomorrow is Saturday, so why don't we meet at your house first thing in the morning and I can have a look at what we're working with. I'm an interior decorator so together we can determine the styles that best work with the house, with your life and with your colors. Then we'll start filling in the blank spaces. What you see here is not anywhere near what we can get. We can also create a gift register for the shower so guests can choose from the list of what you really need and want."

Lana gazed with longing at a lamp shaped like a palm tree. "The problem is, I want it all." The tropical styles of many of the store's pieces struck a cord deep within her, reminding her of one of the happiest times in her life —the few years when she and her mother had lived on Summersby Island. She yearned more than anything to reclaim that sense of home, family, and belonging.

"Does eight o'clock tomorrow work for you?" Mia said. "I know it's early but I have to open here at nine and that should give us time to look around."

The next morning as Lana arrived at her house, Mia pulled up from the other direction. Mack's truck was already backed up to the deck and the house's front door stood wide open. Lana heard the sound of a power saw coming from the interior somewhere and when she and Mia stepped over cords and random bits of boards, they found Mack and one of his crew in the living room cutting baseboard lengths across a couple of sawhorses.

The whining saw stopped and Mack looked up at Lana. His face broke into a smile so wide it startled her.

"Hey," he said. "I didn't expect to see you here this early. Hi, Mia."

"Um, hi," Lana replied. "You two know each other?"

"Sure." Mack answered. "We're both in the business of making houses look good. Besides, we were bound to run into each other sometime on an island this small."

Mia added, "Mack and I have known each other for years, but right now we don't have time for idle chitchat. I have to get back and open the store in less than an hour."

Lana led Mia on a quick tour of the house, discussing color choices and design ideas as they went. Mia took notes on her tablet and snapped photos of the windows and lighting. She gave the 1950s dish on the master bedroom ceiling a dubious look. "Are you planning to get new light fixtures, Lana?" she asked.

"I want to," Lana said, "but I think I need to concentrate on the necessities first, like furniture, drapes or blinds and kitchen things. I will need a table and chairs and some lamps for the living room."

"Are you redoing the kitchen?" Mia asked when they entered the room.

"It's dreadful, isn't it? I can't do it and buy furniture too, so the kitchen is going to have to wait a while. However, I've chosen colors so I can go ahead and get blinds or curtains for the windows. Which do you think I should go with?" Besides the sliding doors leading to the beach patio, the kitchen had one window over the only spot where a table could sit. After some discussion, they agreed that for now, white wide-slat blinds would keep the house cooler and give it the tropical beach look Lana craved. Vertical blinds, also in white, would do for covering the sliding doors for now At some later date she wanted to install hanging louvered plantation-style shutters.

"Well, I've got to run," Mia said, twisting her watch on her arm so she could read the face. "If you want to come by the shop later this afternoon, I'll try to pull together some pieces for you to consider."

After Lana waved her away from the deck, she wandered back into the house. She found Mack down on the floor installing sleek white baseboards in the smaller of the two bedrooms.

"If you've got a minute, would you mind giving me a hand with this?" Mack used the handle of his hammer to indicate where he wanted her to sit.

She dropped to the floor near him. "What happened to your helper?"

"He had another job to do today so it's only you and me. Could you hold this board tight against the wall for me?"

Within a minute Mack had tacked the board on and Lana found herself overshadowed by his body as he moved closer to her. The scent of his aftershave filled her senses. "Thanks," he said.

She stopped looking at the baseboard and instead looked up at him. He set his nail gun on the floor and reached up to lift a strand of her hair away from her face. "Pretty," he said.

Lana smiled at him but didn't say anything.

"You can't imagine how much I want to kiss you right now," Mack said. He waited.

Lana glanced away for a second then met his eyes again. "Why don't you?"

"No reason I can think of." He leaned in. His lips met hers.

A thrill shot through her body and like sheet lightning it lit up all her nerves. *This can't be happening*, her thoughts told her, but then she couldn't think of anything else except the exquisiteness of the moment—the feel, touch, and smell of him.

"Hey! Anybody here?"

Mack and Lana jerked apart, the moment and the thrill of their kiss bursting like a beautiful soap bubble. Heavy boots stomped into the house. Mack jumped to his feet.

"Oh, there y'are." The big freckled face of a grinning man appeared around the doorframe. "I got the bricks ya ordered out here. Where d'ya wann'em?"

Lana watched Mack follow the other man out. She got to her feet, and with one hand against a wall out to steady herself, went to the kitchen and filled the sink with hot water.

No, no, no, said a voice in her head, as she wrung out her washrag. *No, I don't find him attractive. No, this can't go anywhere. No, I can't fall in love again. I can't get hurt again.* But another little voice was saying, *Yes, yes, oh yes*.

The Summersby Island House

Chapter Twelve

After three hours with Mia at Mango Décor, Lana had loaded up both her rental car and her credit card. She decided to keep the window treatments simple until she made final decisions on the furniture, particularly in the living room. She unloaded all her purchases at the house and piled some of the boxes in one of the bedroom closets. Mack wasn't there when she arrived so she texted him to make sure he locked the house when he wasn't around as the furniture had already begun to arrive. Before she could carry everything in, his truck pulled into the driveway and he hopped out.

"Need a hand with anything?" Mack said. Jasper bounded out of the cab after him.

"Hey, Jasper," said Lana. She gave the dog's ears a good scratch. "Are you over your snit? Are you, boy?"

She looked at Mack. "Actually, I've just finished carrying in all the light stuff but you can help with those two tables, if you don't mind."

"Sure thing. Where do you want them?" He grabbed them, followed Lana into the house and put the tables in the small bedroom with everything else.

"The baseboards look nice," she said. She was suddenly aware of Mack's closeness. "You must have finished them…when? While I was at Mango?"

Mack glanced at the baseboards then back at Lana. "About this morning…" He reached toward her and ran the back of one finger down her forearm.

It felt like a burn; a trail of fire singeing her skin.

"Mack, I…"

"Listen, I know you've been through some stuff lately." When she started to protest, he put up both hands. "I want you to know, I get that. I've been through a few things myself and, hey, if you need a friend, you can consider me one. If you want."

His kindness nearly brought tears to Lana's eyes.

"Listen, it's been a long day and we're both supposed to be off work today," Mack said. "Why don't we go home and get cleaned up and I'll take us out to dinner?"

"I'd like that," Lana agreed. She picked up her purse and walked out, locking the door as they left.

Mack arrived at Lana's apartment two minutes before seven o'clock. Not only had he showered, shaved, and dressed in a starched, white shirt and a pair of navy pants, but he'd cleaned the cab of his truck, too. He turned off the ignition and brushed a dog hair from his pant leg, then drew in a long breath as he exited his truck. That's when he spotted the powder blue vintage Vespa parked next to the steps.

Mack rounded the bike, examining every detail from the handlebars to the fenders. "Ohhhh. Beautiful, just beautiful," he murmured.

Lana leaned over the veranda railing. "Thanks," she said. "I washed my hair."

Mack jumped back. "Oh...I didn't mean you."

"No?" Lana pressed her lips together to hide the laughter about to escape, and faked a dejected face.

"Oh, no. I mean, you're beautiful too, but, but the bike..." he stuttered.

Lana laughed out loud. "It's okay. I know when I've been upstaged. Want to go for a spin?"

"Oh, no. No, it's okay. It's sure a beaut, though. Is it yours?"

"Yes. I'll get the keys."

A minute later Lana was back. She found Mack crouched beside the Vespa, scrutinizing the engine.

"Here, catch," Lana said.

"No, you drive. I'll tag along."

Lana's pencil skirt and four-inch heels didn't exactly make getting on the bike easy but she realized it would be a good trial run for riding it to work in her office wear. She turned the key in the ignition as Mack swung a leg over the seat and slid in behind her, wrapping his arms around her waist.

"Hang on," she warned. "I'm a new driver on this."

Off they flew. Ten minutes later they returned, breathless and laughing.

Mack pulled thick stands of auburn hair away from his face as Lana rolled to a stop and shut off the motor. "Man, you have a lot of hair," he said.

"Well, if you hadn't stuck your face in my neck the whole way. Were you scared?" She stepped away from the bike and taunted him with a waggle of her head.

"You bet I was!" Mack laughed as he flipped the helmet off his head. "You scared the living daylights out of me. Come on; let's go to dinner—in my truck. And I'm driving."

At The Island Inn, the island's best and most luxurious restaurant, Mack and Lana shared a table next to a pair of open French doors. The soft sea air, fragrant with the scent of jasmine, kissed the skin on

Lana's bare arms. After a meal of seafood, fresh from the dock, Lana ordered crème brulée, and Mack, his favorite, apple crisp. Over coffee, Mack slid his hand across the white tablecloth and covered Lana's where it lay next to her decimated dessert.

"I wasn't lying, you know," he said.

Lana frowned. "About what?"

"This morning. I wasn't lying about how much I wanted to kiss you. I'm not going to push you into anything you're not ready for but I want you to know that I've wanted to kiss you almost from the first moment I met you." He lifted her fingers and gently pressed his lips to them.

Lana felt her head spinning and her palms begin to perspire. How could she tell him she still felt raw from her abrupt break-up with Carl? That her world was still topsy-turvy from everything that had happened in such a short time—getting let go from the job she loved, being dumped, evicted, moving, buying a house?

"What I'm trying to say," Mack continued, "is that I really like you. I want to see more of you, even after the house is done. However that works for you." He placed another light kiss on her middle knuckle.

Lana gently extricated her hand from his and slid it out of sight to wipe the sweat from her palm. "I can't make any promises," she began. "And right now, I'm so pre-occupied with my new job and the house, and moving…"

"Hey," Mack said, "I recognize a brush off when I hear it." He leaned back in his chair.

"Oh, Mack. I really like you, too. I'm too overwhelmed right now to get involved in a relationship, that's all. Please understand."

"I do," he said, shortly. "I understand."

Lana sensed the curtain coming down on Mack's emotions. She knew enough about men to recognize that too often a "Not right now, thanks" was taken as "Not on your life, buster" by a man. She didn't want that because, as much as the battle raged within her, she couldn't help wanting to be near him. She loved the sight of him, the touch of him, and the scent of him—sawdust and all. There was a kindness about him she found virtually irresistible. In her silence, he turned his head and stared out to sea.

"Can we continue this conversation another day?" Lana leaned into his peripheral vision. "I'm just not ready to make decisions right now."

Mack looked back at her and leaned his elbows on the table. "Listen," he told her, "I said I'm your friend, so for now, why don't we just leave it at that, okay?"

Back at her apartment, Mack handed Lana down from the high truck seat and walked with her up the steps to the door.

"I had a really nice time," she said. She faced him under the porch light. "Thanks again for helping me lug furniture into the house today."

Mack shrugged. "Not a problem. I meant what I said, you know."

"About?"

"About being here if you need me, and…"

"And?"

"About wanting to kiss you." He grasped handfuls of his hair with both hands and threw his head back. "Man, this is hard," he muttered.

Instead of answering, Lana leaned toward him and placed a light kiss on his lips, meaning to stop there. But before she could pull away, his arms encircled her and his mouth demanded more. Her hands moved up his back as though possessed by a force not her own.

Then suddenly Mack tore his lips away. He thrust his fingers into her hair, cupping the back of her head with his hands. Leaning his forehead against hers he said, "I think we'd better leave it at that for now, don't you?"

For one wild, crazy moment, everything in Lana wanted to scream, "Nooo!" but instantly the old familiar panic rose up through her chest and clutched her by the throat. She couldn't abandon herself to the feeling, the terror of possible loss…not again. All she could do was nod.

Mack dropped his hands and looked into her eyes. "You okay?"

Lana drew a breath. "I'm fine."

"All right then. I'll see you tomorrow." Then he turned, bounded down the steps to his truck and with a wave, drove away.

Chapter Thirteen

The canapés were arranged in pretty rows on three separate trays and waited in the refrigerator next to bottles of drinks that would soon be plunged into the big turquoise plastic tub filled with ice resting on the counter. Since the house still had almost no furniture, Lana had asked Sherry to request the guests bring lawn chairs for seating in the living room. The two tables Mack had carried in from the car for her, which were intended as bedside stands, had been forced into duty as coffee tables in the living room for the party.

The kitchen table, dark rattan with a round glass top, sat in the tiny dining room area topped with a splashy, tropical-print cloth. The only chairs Lana owned matched the table and had been set around the room for guest seating should anyone forget, or not have, a lawn chair. Lana had been cleaning all day, trying to make the house presentable. She had moved out of her apartment a few days prior and into her own house.

Her own house. She had to repeat the phrase over and over to get used to the idea. How proud her mother would be to know Lana actually had her own house. They had never owned a home, only moved from one rental to another. Grief and missing her mom always sneaked up on Lana when she least expected, like when she tied a frilly apron on over her skirt a while ago. It was the same apron her mother had always kept for "good," which meant she had hardly ever worn it.

Lana smoothed the fabric down with her hands and checked again that everything was ready. She still felt uncomfortable with the idea of throwing a party for herself in a town where she knew almost no one, but Sherry had insisted that on Summersby Island, it was perfectly acceptable. All the women from the bank had promised to come, and Lana had invited a few ladies from the church she had been attending, even though they were little more than acquaintances.

The doorbell rang and Lana jumped. She pulled the ties on the apron and hung it on a hook inside the broom closet then ran to answer the door. Before she could get there, Sherry burst in, her arms full of gift-wrapped boxes. Several other women came in behind her.

To Lana's surprise and delight, twenty-seven women showed up to help her celebrate home-ownership. Their generosity brought tears to her eyes as she opened gift after gift, most of which came from Mango Décor and had been on her wish list there. By the time they had demolished the refreshments and trouped out the door, waving good-bye and issuing invitations to everything from singing in the church choir to joining a baseball team, Lana felt like part of the community. Sherry lingered to help clean up after everyone else had departed.

"So what's going on with you and Mack?" Sherry asked point blank. She wiped the leftover bottled drinks and loaded them back into the fridge.

Lana felt the heat rise in her cheeks. She tried to evade Sherry's real question. "He's renovating my house, remember?"

"Give me a break! I've seen how the two of you look at each other. He lights up when he lays eyes on you and you go all moony at the sight of him. So, spill it. It's Sherry you're talking to here."

Lana set a tray on the kitchen counter. "I don't know. I think he's fantastic. He's sweet, kind, thoughtful. He doesn't push me. He's…"

"Has he kissed you?"

Lana took a deep breath.

"Enough said," Sherry declared. "I knew there was something going on."

"That's just it, Sher," Lana said. "I'm not sure I want anything to go on. What if he turns out to be another Carl—loves me then leaves me? Or, what if he says he loves me when he really doesn't? I don't think I can do that again."

Sherry moved closer to Lana and gripped her friend's upper arms, staring intently into her eyes. "You have to trust somebody, sometime, Lana. If you don't want to spend the rest of your life alone, you've got to make some choices to change that direction. Mack's a decent guy. Why not go for it?"

Lana looked away, out the window through her new blinds. Outside, where the light from the kitchen fell, she could see the fan palms at the side of her yard. Their stiff fronds twitched in the evening breeze and she watched them for a while, her mind ricocheting through her emotions, bouncing off the hurts, the betrayals, and the pain of loss like a ping-pong ball in a clothes dryer. It all seemed like too much—the lay-off, the sudden decision to move to Summersby Island, taking a new job, buying a house. And then there was Carl. As much as he had torn her heart out, it was like he still owned a part of it. The dreams she had of their future together might be scattered around her feet like shards of broken glass, but she hadn't emptied him out of her system yet. She hadn't had the time to process everything since she moved to Summersby Island. It had all happened too fast.

Sherry gave Lana's arms a gentle shake. "Earth to Lana."

Lana dragged her attention back to the woman standing in front of her. "I'm sorry. I'm just not ready for a relationship with Mack, or with anyone, if it comes down to it. I have enough on my plate right now." She removed Sherry's hands from her arms. "And speaking of plates, let's get these cleaned up. I'm exhausted."

Sherry shrugged. "All right. I can spot a brushoff when I hear one. But I have to say, you're going to have to get your feet wet again one of these days, or you'll spend the rest of your life alone. I don't think you want that."

The following weekend, Lana intended to spend the entire two days arranging her home. The furniture she had ordered had arrived the day before and now stood in disarray in the living room. On Saturday, once she'd removed the cartons from the larger pieces, she stood wondering where the sofa would fit best. Through the window, she saw Mack's truck pull into the drive outside. She watched as he got out, allowing Jasper to bound down after him; then Mack sauntered up the deck steps. He wore khaki knee-length shorts and a tropical print shirt, open at the neck. The sun-bleached hairs on his bronzed arms sparkled in the morning light. His hair was shorter than when she had last seen him the week before. He looked clean and fresh and so good. The window was slightly open so she could hear him command Jasper to lie down on the deck. Then Mack tapped lightly on the front door.

For a fleeting moment, Lana considered not answering. She knew being close to Mack would erode her resolve not to be drawn into the circle of his magnetic manliness. But she couldn't help herself. She walked to the front door and pulled it open. "Hello, Mack."

"Hey," He studied her outfit of cut-off jean shorts and a tank top with the words, *I'm the Queen, I make the Rules*, blazoned across the front. "Uh, nice shirt," he said.

"It was a gift. I can't imagine why."

Mack kept a perfectly straight face. "Yeah, me neither."

"Would you like to come in?"

"Actually, I came to ask if you'd like to come out and play today."

Lana placed a hand on her hip and raised an eyebrow.

"It's a great day for a sail. I've got a little two-person sailing dinghy that can't wait to get out on the water this spring. I was hoping to enlist some crew."

Lana laughed. "What I know about sailing would fit in a thimble. Let me see…there's a boat, and it has a sail. Yep, that's it."

"Not a problem," Mack assured her. "What I know about sailing would fill an encyclopedia. Come with me. Please."

"As lovely as that sounds, I've got a house full of freshly unloaded furniture to get out of crates and moved into place. I can't come out and play today."

Mack mugged a crestfallen expression, then his face lit up. "I know. Why don't we work together on your house? It will go twice as fast. Then we can both kick back and go sailing. What do you say?"

Lana felt like she had stepped into a current too swift for her and had been knocked off her feet. She really did need help with the house and to turn him down would be rude. Besides, the prospect of spending the afternoon sailing around the island was too delicious to refuse. On the other hand, she knew spending more time with Mack meant she would be treading in dangerous emotional waters and she wasn't sure she was up to it.

"Pleeeeeese," Mack said, begging like a child. He got down on his knees and took her hand, kissing it repeatedly. Jasper leapt to his feet, barked and jumped around with excitement and licked Lana's other hand—repeatedly.

"Oh, for heaven's sake," Lana said. "Would you two cut it out, already? All right, come on in. I could use the help and yes, I'll go sailing with you, on one condition."

Mack jumped to his feet. "What's that?"

"You keep that crazy dog of yours from licking my hand off."

Mack followed her inside. She hadn't said anything about him not kissing her hand off.

Chapter Fourteen

The sunlight sparkled in the wavelets in the bay like fragments of the stars had fallen from the sky and now bobbed on the water's surface. The wind was light, according to Mack, indicating easy sailing. Lana sat in the bow of the tiny boat with her legs curled under her, leaning against the backrest of a small seat. The boat itself was hardly bigger than a rowboat and had one sail and a tiller that Mack handled while he directed the craft away from DiMarco's Marina and into the coastal waters. Jasper lay at Lana's feet watching every move Mack made as though he were taking sailing lessons.

Once underway, the little boat skimmed across the waves, as light as a skating leaf, while the wind tangled Lana's hair. She pulled it back into a ponytail and twisted a band around it. The shores of Summersby Island gradually receded and the silence of the open water overtook them. Except for the screeches of occasional gulls investigating the scavenging opportunities, all Lana could hear was the slap of the water against the bow and the snap of the sail in the wind. Mack's attention, riveted on the job of manoeuvring the boat at first, soon turned to the joy of sailing. She could read it in his eyes, and the way his muscular tanned arms worked at directing the boat.

With her big, round sunglasses on, she thought she could get away with watching him without him realizing it but when he looked her way, he smiled.

"Having fun?" he asked.

"This is amazing! I've never sailed like this before."

"I thought you used to live on the island."

"I did, but it wasn't for very long and I only went out on the water in a sailboat once, when a school friend had a birthday party. That seems like eons ago now."

"Would you like me to teach you how to sail?"

Lana thought about it for a moment. "Yes, but not right now. I'm pooped from heaving furniture around so I probably wouldn't be able to absorb anything you say."

Mack nodded. "Next time we go out, I'll start showing you the ropes...so to speak."

Lana felt warmed by his assumption that there would be a next time. He angled away from her to adjust something at the boat's stern and she could she the muscles of his shoulders ripple beneath his chambray shirt. *Oh my*, she thought, *I sure like this guy*. Maybe he wasn't like all the rest. Maybe he was not the kind of guy who thought of leaving when another woman in a skirt walked past. Sherry had told her Mack's fiancé had ditched him at the altar but Mack had never told Lana anything about it himself. Suddenly, she had to know. She needed to know everything about him she could. Her heart might not be able to be trusted, but her head was still screwed on straight.

She tried to word the request as gently as possible in case she touched a raw nerve. "Mack, please tell me about your, um, your unfortunate wedding experience."

He twisted his body toward her and leaned his elbows on his knees. For a moment, he stared down at Jasper who looked up as though he also wanted to hear what Mack had to say. The dog glanced toward Lana then back at Mack.

"Shayla and I met in Tampa at a birthday party for a friend of mine. It was one of those things where you see someone across a crowded room. Yeah, I know, it sounds pretty hokey, but it was the truth. Almost from the moment we met, we were inseparable. It was like we were made for each other and we knew it. She was a marine architect and engineer and worked for a boat-building firm and I was struggling to get my own business off the ground. I guess you could say I fell hard for her and I thought it was mutual. When I asked her to marry me, she said 'yes' and started planning this outlandish wedding. I wanted to get married on the beach with a few friends and family. She wanted the society shindig of the century, with nine bridesmaids, if you can believe that." He reached down and scratched Jasper's ears and the dog lay his head down with a contented sigh.

"How long were you engaged?"

"Just over a year. Shayla said you had to book all the venues that far in advance or you'd never get the church or the hotel ballroom for the date you wanted. Now that I think back on it all, it was like I unwittingly climbed aboard a speeding train and couldn't get off. She and her mother and sisters orchestrated the engagement party, the rehearsal dinner and all that fancy stuff. By the time the wedding day arrived, I felt like a bit player in the movie of my own life."

"So what happened?"

"I had my tux on and was waiting in this little room in the church for the wedding planner to give me and the guys the go-ahead to make our entrance when Shay came running in, insisting she had to talk to me." Mack's shoulders bunched up and he looked away, staring out across the water. "The guys made an exit so we could be alone. That's when she told me she couldn't go through with it. Apparently, it wasn't what she wanted after all. She didn't tell me at the time, but she'd decided to take a job in California and she had met someone she thought was a better fit for her lofty opinion of her social station—a plastic surgeon!" He spat out the words like they tasted rancid. "I guess a humble carpenter wasn't up to her standards." He looked at Lana. "And that's about all there was to it. Her parents were furious. They'd spent buckets of money. I think her folks genuinely felt bad for me."

"I'm so sorry."

"Don't be. In retrospect, I'm thankful now she didn't go through with it. She wanted a different kind of life than I did. Who knows where we'd be today if we had actually gotten married?"

Lana reached out and placed her hand on Mack's. "Life can be pretty disappointing sometimes, can't it?"

He placed his other hand over hers, trapping it in his hold. "You know it too, don't you?"

"Yeah," she said, ruefully.

"But hey, today is a beautiful day. We're out sailing on a turquoise sea and right now, all is well with the world, right?"

By now they had rounded the north end of the island and sailed in a wide curve that would take them back to the marina. The turquoise waters had begun to turn teal in the lowering light and would soon be followed by navy blue, then would light up with a brilliant splash of mango-lemon fizz as the sun sizzled into the waiting sea.

A lone gull had been circling the sailboat and chose that moment to dive down and land awkwardly on the bow of the boat. Jasper exploded from his curled up dozing position on the floor and lunged for the bird, barking furiously. He hurdled over Lana's left shoulder in a blur of black and white fur. The gull gave one squawk and lifted off in a single wing flap and Jasper leaped after it. The bird flew off unperturbed but Jasper had caught his hind leg in a coil of rope. Lana heard a soft snap as Jasper plunged into the water and his alarmed yelp rang out. Floundering and crying, he struggled to stay afloat as the distance between him and the sailboat grew. The rope that had snagged his leg now drifted deeper into the dark water, no longer connected with Jasper's leg.

Mack cranked the tiller. "Jasper! He's hurt!" The little boat swooped in a tight curve as the sail came about. "We have to get him!"

As soon as the boat drew near the dog, Mack shouted "Grab this and lean away from me as hard as you can "

Lana stuttered, "I…I don't know how to sail!"

"Just do as I say," Mack barked. "You'll be fine."

Mack hooked his heels under the opposite gunwale and leaned on his belly as far out as his body would reach. "Come on, Jasper," he called. "Come on, boy."

The boat edged closer to the dog as Jasper battled against the drag of the water. With each breath he howled in pain. In another moment, they had reached Jasper and with one mighty swing of his strong arms, Mack swept the quivering animal into his arms. "It's okay, boy. Hold on, Jasper." He crooned softly as he twisted his body and dragged both himself and his pet into the boat. Mack placed the shivering dog gently on the floor and carefully examined him while Jasper turned pleading eyes toward Lana.

Tears spilled down Lana's cheeks as she watched Mack check each of the dog's limbs.

"His leg is broken," Mack said. "I think it's his fibula but I can't be sure." He glanced up at Lana. "I need you to help keep him calm while I get us back to town. If you've got your cell with you, can you call Dr. Keen so she'll be waiting at the clinic when we get there?"

Lana changed places with Mack in the rocking boat and followed his instructions. Jasper's damp head rested on her lap as she called the vet who agreed to meet them, even though it was after hours. Twenty minutes later they had docked the boat and Mack begged a sailing pal at the marina to take care of it. Mack lifted Jasper out of the craft and ran to the truck. Lana pulled a blanket from behind the front seat and laid it in the back of the vehicle where she rode with Jasper while Mack tore through the streets to the clinic.

"He'll have to stay the night," Dr. Keen, a robust forty-something woman with short brown hair and straight-forward manner, informed Mack after she had treated and put a cast on the dog's leg. "He's sedated and won't wake up until morning. Then we'll see how he gets around."

Mack and Lana were silent on the ride back to her house on the beach. Once Mack parked, they got out and he walked with her to the front door.

Lana said, "Would you like to come in for a while? I can make some coffee."

Mack leaned against the wall next to the door and shook his head. He gave her a weary smile. "I don't think so. It's been a pretty full day."

"You really love him, don't you? Jasper, I mean."

"Yeah, he's a great dog."

She lifted her hand to touch the side of Mack's face and he grasped it and kissed her palm. Then his eyes met hers. "I really love you, too, you know. There, I've said it."

"Oh, Mack…"

"It's okay," he said. "You don't have to say anything. I can wait."

"I…"

He let her hand go and reached toward her. Cupping her face with both his hands, he leaned in and kissed her lips. As he pulled away, all he said was, "Ssshh. We'll talk tomorrow."

Lana watched as he tramped down the deck steps, got into his truck, and drove away. Before he was out of sight, she saw his hand lift in a tired wave. Then he was gone.

Chapter Fifteen

By Monday morning, Mack still hadn't contacted her like he had promised. Lana ached to call him. She'd even picked up the phone half a dozen times every hour, but talked herself out of it each time. Mack's words tumbled around in her head and caught in her throat over and over. He had told her he loved her.

Oh, how she wanted to believe Mack. She wanted him to love her, but she didn't want him to. Plagued by her own uncertainty, she went through the motions of getting ready for church, singing the worship songs, listening to the sermon she now couldn't remember, and greeting people as though she was actually there. Her heart was on its own quest and she had no idea what it would find.

She couldn't help comparing Mack with Carl even though Mack was as different from Carl as denim is to silk. It wasn't that she clung to any hope of ever seeing Carl again. It was over with him. But, was she ready to let herself fall for Mack?

Yes. No. Maybe.

Lana spend the rest of Sunday ordering her house and scrubbing cupboards, hoping to keep her mind off waiting for the phone to ring. Around five o'clock she tossed down her rubber gloves and headed for the beach, her cell phone in her pocket. She walked half way down the length of the island before she lifted her head and realized how far she had gone. Reluctantly, she turned back toward home.

Home. She finally had what she had longed for her entire life. Home. It was hers to keep—a place from which no one could evict her because they had other plans for the space or because the rent wasn't paid. A place she didn't have to leave because she knew there was a cheaper, and shabbier, apartment across town. She really did have a place to put down roots and make her very own. Why, then, did she still feel such a big hollow space in her chest? Her own home was meant to fill that empty cavity, wasn't it?

She trudged along the water's edge, gazing out across the sea as it rippled away toward the flame and lavender sunset.

On Monday morning, Lana parked her scooter behind the bank and switched from her flip flops to a pair of leopard-print kitten heels before entering the bank. She found Owen Sheffield talking with Sally McCardle in the back hallway.

Lana greeted them briefly then headed straight for her office.

"I hear you've got a thing going on with one of your clients." Owen's sly, taunting voice called after her. Lana froze. "Could get sticky."

She spun around. Lana couldn't have cared less what Owen thought of her or her personal choices, but her manager's opinion mattered. She flung a withering glance in Owen's direction then stole a cautious one at Sally's face. To Lana's relief, Sally's raspberry red lips curved up in a smile.

"Pay no attention to him," Sally said. She placed a firm hand on Owen's shoulder and prodded him toward his office. "Just keep everything above board, Lana. That's all I ask."

"Don't worry, we're just friends," Lana assured her. But Lana was not entirely clear if that were the case or if there was a lot more to it.

"I saw Mack leaving on the ferry yesterday morning. Where's he off to?" Sally asked.

Lana replied as evenly as she could manage. "I, uh, have no idea. Perhaps he has work there."

By noon, Lana couldn't handle the suspense any longer. She pulled her cell phone out of her purse and texted Mack an innocuous message.

Haven't heard from you. Hope Jasper is okay.

A couple of minutes later she got a reply.

Leg in cast. He's fine. Picking up lumber. Gotta run.

Lana sighed. At least Mack had answered. She knew if he left yesterday and was picking up lumber today, it could only mean he had a contract on the mainland. And that could only mean he might be gone a while.

The remainder of the week dragged by. On Thursday evening, Lana cooked a plate of Fettuccini Alfredo and tossed a green salad. She took her dinner out to the tiny table she had placed on the patio and ate, watching the daylight fade. Half way through her meal she found herself staring out at the ocean, thinking about Mack. Maybe he was not like all the rest. After all, there had to be *some* good guys out there. He seemed to be ready to settle into a relationship. But was she? Perhaps he thought she had come along at the right time for him but just because it was right for him didn't mean it would be right for her. Could she let go of her fear that kept him at arm's length? Her thoughts went round and round. After a while, she put her fork down on her pale blue napkin.

Lana pushed her patio chair back and rose to her feet. She walked across the sand to the water's edge and stood there for a long while, gazing out to sea until the turmoil in her mind began to wane with the gentle rhythm of the waves rolling onto the sand. She slipped off her sandals and, one foot at a time, stepped into the water. She knew she did not want to spend the rest of her life alone. She looked down and watched as the warm gulf water covered her feet up to her ankles. They were wet.

On Friday morning, she couldn't stand wondering any more. She texted a short message to Mack asking if he'd be on the island for the weekend. He didn't answer.

The day dragged by as Lana tried to distract herself with paperwork while periodically glancing up at the clock as the hands crept toward five o'clock. Finally, she shut down her computer and picked up her purse. She said goodnight to her co-workers and headed out the back door to her scooter. The weather promised to be fair, as usual, so maybe she would tour the island on her bike and see what had changed since she had lived there so many years before.

Lana tucked her hair into an elastic band before slipping on her helmet. She looked up to see a man leaning against a shiny black Escalade. He had one designer loafer-clad foot crossed over the other and his arms were folded casually across his chest. She recognized those shoes.

"Hi, baby," he said. He pushed away from the vehicle.

Lana froze, her helmet halfway to her head. When she could breathe again she managed to squeak, "What are you doing here, Carl?"

Carl strolled toward her, his hips moving in that way that used to drive her wild when she watched him walk away down the hallway at work. "I came to see you, of course."

"Why?" She frowned.

"Don't be like that," he said. "This is a friendly visit. My folks are at their place in Kissimmee and I came down for a break. I heard you were here, so I came to invite you to come and do the parks with me for the weekend."

"The parks?" Lana's dazed brain couldn't make sense of his words. "What parks?"

"Disney World, Universal Studios? You know, the amusement parks. My folks can't wait to see you again. We can stay at their house. You'll like it there."

Lana shook her head and hung her helmet over the handlebar of her scooter. "What happened to your new girlfriend?" she asked stiffly. "Why don't you take her?"

Carl glanced away. "Oh, she's history. That was nothing." He looked back at Lana and took a step closer. "You must know it's always been you I love."

She scowled at him. "You have a funny way of showing it, Carl. You dump me the same day the company fires me. I got evicted from my apartment, too, so they could sell it. You didn't care in the least a few months ago. Now you want me to go and play with you for the weekend? I don't think so." But even as she said it, she felt her resolve melting. All throughout her childhood she had longed to visit Disney World, but her mother never had the means to take them there. The old longing for what she could never have rose up in her chest. Carl could give her things like this, any time. And she would love to see his parents again.

"Lana, I'm simply asking you to come have a little fun with me this weekend. If, after that, you never want to see me again, so be it. I want another chance to show you I'm not such a bad guy. I really do care about you. I've realized that. But we don't even have to go there, if you don't want to. Just let me take you to the parks so we can have some fun."

Lana felt her resistance disintegrating to dust and drifting to the pavement around her feet. The longing for all the things she'd never had overpowered her and she blinked to keep her eyes from misting over.

"All right, Carl," she said. "Just this weekend. I would like to see your parents again."

Carl grinned so widely his back teeth showed. "That's great, baby. We can leave right away and catch the next ferry. Where do you live?"

Chapter Sixteen

An hour later, Lana stood next to Carl on the ferry to the mainland, looking out across the water. Still not sure she was doing the right thing, she fought the old feelings she had had for him. And she couldn't help thinking about having stood at this same railing with Mack not two weeks before.

They ate an early dinner at a Mexican restaurant outside Sarasota and arrived at Carl's parents' home after dark. Janet and Carl Jenkins—the second— greeted Lana with genuine warmth, inviting her into their lavish vacation home. After drinks on the terrace by the pool, Lana was shown to a guest room, down the hall from Carl's, and wished a good sleep.

By the first light of dawn, Lana finally gave up all hope of a restful night. She had drifted in and out of unquiet sleep and bizarre dreams, finding no comfort. A while later, Carl tapped on her door.

"Hey, Lan, are you awake?"

Lana rolled out of bed and opened the door.

"Hi, beautiful," he said. He kissed her cheek. "Let's get an early start. There is a lot of fun to be had today. Breakfast is ready."

"I'll be down in fifteen minutes, if that's okay."

Carl agreed and closed the door as Lana headed for the shower.

Over breakfast, Janet, Carl's mother, rested her hand on Lana's arm. "It's wonderful to have you with us again, dear," she said. "I've missed seeing you." She flicked a glance in her son's direction and Lana saw his face redden.

"I can second that," Carl Senior added. "Now that this boy is getting his head screwed on straight again, I hope we'll be seeing a lot more of you."

"I've missed seeing you both, too," said Lana. She gave Carl Senior a weak smile and looked down at her plate. She genuinely liked these people. How could she say no?

Carl and Lana spent the day at Disney World, barely scratching the surface of everything there was to do. They thrilled to the rides, ate ridiculously unhealthy foods and loved them all, and walked until their feet ached. In the evening, Carl took Lana to a quiet restaurant where they shared a meal.

Each time Carl tried to bring up their past relationship, Lana cut him off. "That was then; this is now," she informed him. "Besides, I'm exhausted and if we're going to Universal Studios tomorrow, I need a good night's sleep."

The next morning, Lana got up early, dressed, and found Janet having coffee on the deck before Carl and his father appeared.

"Come and sit here with me," Janet said. She poured a cup of coffee for Lana. "I love this time of day, before it gets hot. I saw an egret this morning right over there." She pointed to a spot near the small fountain and pond at the bottom of the property. "It's beautiful here, don't you think? I'm trying to talk Carl into moving down here permanently but he's not ready."

Lana slid into a rattan chair next to the glass-topped table. She took a sip of her coffee.

"What's happening with you and my son, Lana?" While Janet was always gracious, she never beat around bushes. "I think he's seen the error of his ways concerning you."

"I don't know, Janet. I left Chicago because everything in my life there collapsed at once. I lost my job, my apartment, and the man I thought I loved, all on the same day. It felt like God was sending me a message…time to leave town. When I got the opportunity to move to Summersby Island, I took it, having no other prospects in hand. I just wanted to get away and start over." Lana took another drink from her cup. She knew Janet was watching her. "Did you know I've bought a house?"

Janet hesitated. "No, I hadn't heard. Does that mean you're planning to stay on the island?"

"For now."

Janet placed her fingers on Lana's arm, a loving gesture Lana had once cherished. "You know I would love to have you for my daughter-in-law. Before you left Chicago, I thought we would be making wedding plans soon."

"I thought so too," Lana said.

"Maybe it's not too late."

Lana didn't answer because she didn't know what to say. Maybe it wasn't too late.

The Universal Studios Park opened at 9:00 a.m. and Carl and Lana were near the front of the line-up to get in. Once they had passed through the gates, Carl grabbed Lana's hand and they raced from ride to ride. Their stomachs lurched on the virtual reality rides and on the rollercoasters they both screamed with excitement. As they staggered out of the Spiderman amusement, Carl suggested, "Let's go for a drink. I need to stop my head from spinning."

They took their drinks to a shady spot. "I owe you an apology," Carl said. "What I did to you in Chicago was, frankly, unconscionable. It was stupid, and I have no excuses, except to say sometimes I do stupid things. Can you forgive me?" He reached for her hand and took her fingers in his.

"I forgave you some time ago," Lana replied. "I learned early on in my life that carrying unforgiveness does far more harm to me than to anyone else. You did what you did for your own reasons and I can't change that."

"You make it sound so final. What I'm saying is, I made a mistake. It was a doozy, too."

A young mother pushing a stroller with a sleeping baby walked past. She held the hand of small boy with pink candy all over his face. The little boy chattered happily to his mother and she answered back. The tall father followed, carrying a toddler on his shoulders. Lana watched the little family as they strolled out of sight. Finally, she said, "What is it you want now, Carl?"

"Isn't it obvious? I want you back. Come on, baby. What do you say? Can we start again?"

She stared at him. Tall, good-looking in an executive sort of way, he epitomized a man with a great future. She knew if she said yes, she could see exactly what the years ahead would hold. They would have a couple of children who would attend a private school. Thanksgiving and Christmas would be at Janet and Carl Sr.'s house, which would be decked out in the latest decorator styles and colors. The children would play football, or study ballet, take piano lessons, or learn to play the flute. They would attend Ivy League colleges. Lana would entertain lavishly, especially Carl's clients and work colleagues. They would be members of the country club and she would wear each season's new designer trends. From where she sat outside an ice cream shop at Universal Studios, it looked like a pretty good life. If she tried, she could imagine being Carl's wife.

She swept a hand up to pull her hair away from her neck and instead caught her drink glass, sending it clattering to the street and spilling iced tea all over the table and off its edge.

"Oh, no!" She leaped up and grabbed for the thin napkins on the table. She mopped furiously at the spilled liquid, trying to keep it away from her white pants. Carl sat where he was and handed her another napkin. A moment later, an attendant arrived and took over.

Carl stood up and pushed his chair back. "Come on," he said. "He can take care of the rest. Let's go."

Lana followed Carl, almost running to keep up. Eventually, Carl slowed enough for her to fall in step with him.

"I'm sorry, Carl," Lana said. "That was bad timing."

"I noticed." He took her hand and kept walking.

Together, they went on a few more rides but Lana finally admitted to herself she wasn't having any fun. Her head ached and her feet throbbed. They ate lunch at a busy bistro that didn't invite intimate conversation. By the time they had finished and left the restaurant it was nearly two o'clock.

"I think we should head back now," Lana said. She squinted in the bright sunshine. "I have to work tomorrow and it will take us a few hours to get back to the island."

"I guess you're right," Carl conceded. "We'll stop by the house and pick up your things. I know my folks will want to see you again before we go."

At Carl's parents' home, Lana gathered her things and said good-bye to her hosts.

"Please come and see us again," Janet begged. "Stay longer next time. We'll go shopping together, just us girls."

Carl Sr. leaned toward her and squeezed her arm. "And we'll have supper at the club."

Chapter Seventeen

The ferry was starting to load by the time they reached the dock. Lana had fallen asleep almost before Carl had steered his big SUV onto the freeway toward Sarasota. She woke at the ticket booth for the ferry.

Once on board, Carl took Lana's elbow and helped her climb the stairs to the upper deck where they stood by the railing again and watched as the craft pulled away from land.

"Can we talk?" Carl asked. He turned Lana toward him and wrapped his arms around her.

"Of course."

"I tried to tell you this earlier but, well, it wasn't the best time. I want you to know I was a fool to allow you to leave. I didn't know what I had until it was too late." He nuzzled the side of her neck. "Say you'll come back to me. You can keep your house here on the island. We'll use it for our vacations."

Despite her fatigue and jumbled emotions, Lana *could* imagine them having vacations on the beach here on Summersby, with their children playing in the sand out past the patio. "I suppose we could try again," she said. "There are some things we'll have to get straight though."

"There's no one else for me. I learned my lesson."

"That's good." A man walked by carrying two little girls, each dressed in leggings and t-shirts and with their brown curly hair in pigtails. "That could be us in a few years," Lana said softly.

"Huh?" said Carl.

"With a couple of children. We never talked about having a family before, Carl. You do want kids, don't you?" She searched his face.

He grinned nonchalantly. "Sure, baby, whatever you want. If you want kids, we'll have a couple of them."

Once they were on Summersby Island and had made their way to Sandpiper road, Carl parked the SUV in Lana's driveway. "Let me grab your bag," he said. He followed her to the door.

"I'm sorry, you can't stay here," Lana told him. "But The Island Inn is only a five minute drive away."

Carl set her bag on the floor in the front hallway. "No problem. I have to head back to Chicago tomorrow so I'm going to stay in Tampa tonight. Why don't you grab some more of your things and come with me?"

Lana's eyes widened. "You didn't tell me that. I thought you were staying with your parents for a while."

Carl shrugged. "Something came up at the office and I have to take care of it. But I'll be back down next weekend. You can come with me then if you'd rather." He wrapped his arms around Lana and drew her close. His lips met hers and kissed her with the same passion she used to know from him. Nothing in his kiss had changed. She would marry him and they would build a life together. As his lips moved over hers she waited for the familiar thrill to course down her body, that quiver of ecstasy she used to experience in his arms. But this time, it never came. Thoughts whirled through her brain. *I could marry him, I could marry him.* Finally, when he pulled away and looked into her eyes, she knew.

"I can't go with you, Carl."

"What? Come on, baby." He looked like she had punched him in the gut.

"I'm sorry but it would never work."

"What are you talking about? On the ferry you said we could start over again. We'll get married; we'll have a couple of kids. I told you things will be different this time."

"Stop," she said. She stepped away from his embrace. "I can't marry you, Carl. When you kissed me just now, I knew. I can't talk myself into being in love with you, no matter how many promises you make or how many country club memberships you get. I can't marry you, Carl, because I don't love you. I used to love you…I think, but I don't anymore."

"I can't believe you're saying this, that you're doing this to me."

Lana shook her head. "I'm not doing it to you, Carl. I'm doing it for me. I want to be loved, not just be a wife. There is a difference."

He stared at Lana silently for a few moments then sighed deeply. "If that's the way you feel about it, there's not much I can do. It's going to break my mother's heart, though."

Lana couldn't believe it. Did he seriously believe pleasing his mother was going to make her want him? "I think you'd better go now," she said.

Carl walked out the door, got in his vehicle and drove away, all without a backward glance.

Lana closed the door and went into the kitchen for a cold drink. At the doorway, she stopped. The room before her was nothing like the kitchen she had left only two days before. The entire room had been transformed—the cabinets, the countertops, the sink, the flooring, everything! What had happened? The place was spotless and brand new. On the counter next to the sink lay an open magazine. She stepped closer and recognized it immediately as the picture of her dream kitchen, which had come to life before her eyes. Her hands flew to her mouth as she twirled in a circle and studied everything. She walked over to the sliding glass doors with new blinds hanging to one side, so she could view the room from a different angle.

She glanced out to the patio and with a jolt realized she was looking at a pair of men's work boots at the end of long, blue-jean-clad legs. As she pulled open the sliding door her gaze followed the legs up and settled on Mack's face. His eyes were closed but when she stepped out onto the patio, he opened one of them.

"I was going to get you to help me hang those blinds," he said, "but when you weren't here, I had to do it myself."

Tears sprang into Lana's eyes. "You did all this?" She swallowed the lump in her throat. "How…?"

At the sound of Lana's voice, Jasper got to his feet and hobbled over to her, his hind leg in the cast tapping the patio stones with each step.

Mack sat up and leaned forward, his elbows on his knees. "I was going to tell you about it on Friday. I thought it would be fun to work together installing the cabinets and everything. But when you weren't home, I called Sherry to see if she knew where you'd gone. She told me you'd gone to the mainland for the weekend, and since I still have the key to your house, I decided I might as well get to work while you were gone." He tilted his head and looked up at her. "Do you like it?"

"Oh, Mack," she cried. "I love it. It's the kitchen I've always wanted. It's as beautiful as I imagined. No, more beautiful. But how did you…?"

"I spent all week at a pal's shop on the mainland, building the cabinets to spec. I got one of my guys to put in some overtime for me to put them in and we got the flooring down this morning. You really like it?" He got to his feet and stuck his thumbs into his jeans pockets.

Lana brow furrowed. "But I can't pay you."

Mack shook his head. "I'm not asking you to. It's a gift. I wanted to give you a dream come true."

A sob broke from Lana's throat and she threw her arms around his neck. "I can't ever thank you enough." She cried into the front of his plaid cotton shirt. "I don't even know what to say."

"How about this? Say you'll marry me." Mack kissed her forehead. "Say you'll stay with me forever. We'll have a bunch of little kids who'll get to grow up on the beach. We'll add onto the house every time we have another baby. I know a good contractor."

Lana sniffed and wiped the tears from her cheeks with the heels of her hands. "Marry you? Yes! Have babies? Definitely."

Mack kissed her, long and slowly. "About building onto the house," she said when he finally pulled back to look at her. "With all those babies, I think we'll have to. I happen to know a good loans officer at the bank."

"That's good," Mack said, "because we're going to need those extra rooms." He kissed her again. "Now, let's go for a walk and talk about the wedding. Maybe we should get married right here on our beach. Would you like that?" Lana nodded and smiled as

Mack draped his arm across her shoulders and they set off toward the water's edge.

The sun hovered above the surface of the water and shot brilliant rays of light across the waves. Behind them the Summersby Island house reflected back its radiance.

Wendy Dewar Hughes and Suzanne Lieurance

BOOKS BY WENDY DEWAR HUGHES

Available in Print
and E-book

Available in Print
and E-book

Available in Print
and E-book

Available in Print
and E-book

Available in E-book Only

Available in Print
and E-book

Available in Print

Available in Print
and E-book

Available in Print
and E-book

Subscribe to Creative Inspirations Daily at
www.wendydewarhughes.com.

BOOKS BY SUZANNE LIEURANCE

Available at www.morning-nudge-book.com
For daily emails, subscribe to The Morning Nudge at
www.morningnudge.com.